By Addison Creek

The Rhinestone Witches
Pointy Hats and Witchy Cats
Rhinestone Way
Pointy Shoes and Cauldron Blues

Witch of Mintwood Series
Witch Way to Mintwood
Witch Some Win Some
Spell by Midnight
A Witch on Mintwood Mountain
Witch Raising Situation
Witch Way Round
Witch Wish Way
White Witch Wonder
Muddled Mintwood Murderer
Wonder Wand Way
Miraculous Mintwood Magic

Witch of Mintwood Mysteries 1-3
Witch of Mintwood Mysteries 4-6
Witch of Mintwood Mysteries 7-9

Witchy Minter Wonderland

The Jane Garbo Mysteries
Spooky Business
Spooky Spells
Spooky Spider
Spooky Spindle
Spooky Skeleton
Spooky Scarecrow

Spooky Business

(The Jane Garbo Mysteries, Book 1)

by

Addison Creek

Join Addison Creek's mailing list:
https://addisoncreek.wordpress.com/

Table of Contents

Chapter One

"I regret to inform you that your contract has been terminated," said my boss, a thin man with a thin face, pale eyes, and a receding hairline.

"What does that mean?" I said.

We were having a frantic week, and I'd scarcely had time to breathe since a new contract came in. I had been working day and night, and come late afternoon I didn't have any energy for mysteries.

I didn't love my job. I just couldn't afford to lose it.

"It means you are no longer an employee here. Your desk is being packed as we speak. Please collect your things." He was already looking down at his desk, intently examining the latest report on something unimportant.

My boss was calm, but I was in shock. I barely caught myself in time to keep my wrist from twitching. Magic in front of a human was not allowed, even a scaly reptilian excuse for a human like this one.

"Can you tell me why I was terminated?" I choked out. Didn't they need a reason to fire me? Like, I'd made the copy machine erupt in flames or something like that?

Just for the record, that wasn't me. That was my story and I was sticking to it.

"You're late to work too much," my boss informed me, his lips tight.

"I've been late once and it was by three minutes," I countered. This was true. I was a stickler for being on time. Probably because in my youth you never wanted to be late to feed an angry ghost.

"Yes, well, I don't believe that's entirely accurate," he huffed. Then he looked away again.

"Pretty sure it is," I informed him. He'd already fired me. There wasn't much more to lose.

He glared at me. "Are you calling me a liar?"

"Only if you're calling me late." I braced my hands on my hips.

I was rolling along in the conversation at this point. I wasn't going to go down without a fight.

"What about that time Cynthia's lunch went missing?" he demanded.

"That wasn't me," I argued.

"Prove it," he said.

"She always gets cucumbers in her sandwiches. I hate them," I said.

"A likely story," he countered.

I rubbed my forehead hard. "You can't just fire me," I said desperately.

"Why are you doing that?" My boss looked confused and concerned.

"What?" I kept rubbing.

He shook his head. "Fine," he said. "But there was also the incident with the copy machine."

He watched me closely and must have read the defeat on my face. With a tight smile, he signaled that he knew he'd won, but I stood there for so long that he felt the need to say more.

"You can't possibly be upset. You must know how to handle this. Haven't you been fired a bunch of times now?" His guilt must have been kicking in.

"Does that mean you aren't firing me?" I asked hopefully.

"I'm definitely firing you," he said. He was no longer guilty. He just wanted me gone. "Fired."

So, I was out of work.

Again.

If I didn't find another job soon, something worse than death would happen.

My hand found its way to my forehead again.

It was going to happen. I just knew it. Every time I got fired, like clockwork, it happened.

But this time would be different.

This time I'd have to go home.

Outside, the night was buzzing. Not with natural sounds, but with the sounds of city life. Cars racing past, the honking of a horn, music blaring from a high-rise.

I went back to my shoebox of an apartment.

My three roommates were out clubbing.

Again.

I stared at the blinking light on my answering machine for a long time. There was only one person who would call my landline, because there was only one reason I had a landline.

I had a landline at the insistence of the person I feared most in all the world, the person we all, in my family, felt the need to obey.

Mother.

Blink, blink, blink.

My face felt hot and my willpower weakened as the minutes stretched on. My hand would twist to press the on button, then I'd find my resolve again and pull it back.

No way was I going to listen to the message just because she'd called me.

She wasn't the boss of me anymore. I could stand on my own. That's why I lived in the city now.

Wrenching myself away from the phone, I went to the kitchen, found a quart of chocolate ice cream, and started eating it. Passing back through the hallway with the ice cream in my hands, I couldn't avoid seeing the flashing message light again.

My hands were sweaty from the need to persevere, and cold from holding the ice cream.

Message, message, message.

She didn't even have the courtesy to text instead of calling, sure proof that she wasn't a good person.

I kept walking.

I could resist her nonsense!

I was halfway to the living room when my legs started to shake and I had to admit that I couldn't.

Who was I kidding? Mom always won in the end.

My eyes squeezed tightly shut. I pressed the button.

"Hi, Jane, we could really use some help with the house this season. Let me know when you can get a train home. Rose, STOP that, damnit! Cookie, why are you encouraging her! You know how much Audrey hates it when Rose jumps on the counter!"

I covered my face with my hands and kept listening.

"Is that Jane?" an older voice crackled out. "Tell her to get her butt home! What job could be better than putting up with you people here?" Cookie's voice was distant but still as sharp as Rose's claws.

My mother battled through it to keep leaving her message.

"Jane, right, am I still leaving a message? Is this thing on?" *Tap tap tap.* "I tried calling before and it was like the answering machine was unplugged. Very strange. Anyway, come home! See you soon!"

"We could really use your help at the SpookyBooSpectacular," Cookie gurgled gleefully.

My shoulders slumped.

I didn't even bother to delete the message.

The need to pack took me into the bathroom. The third time I passed the mirror I made the mistake of looking.

My options were limited. They were actually non-existent. There was just the one left.

There it was.

Right there on my forehead: a monster zit. The stress had set in.

I was going home.

The sun was up but the day was still cool as I headed for the train station. I got plenty of strange looks as I lugged my old trunk along the street. Okay, sure, it had once belonged to a vampire, and it had stickers on it that said things like "Blood is good" in big lurid letters. But why should people judge?

I did my best to hide my luggage once I was seated on the train. The conductor came by and gave me a funny look, so I used my heel to shove it even further out of view. Then I pressed my forehead to the cool window glass and tried to prepare myself for what was coming.

The trees flew by. Occasionally a house jumped into the mix, but then it too streaked past the window. The train was empty the next morning, but I knew it would fill up as the ride went on.

After one stop to let passengers on and off, a man wearing a top hat and a sullen expression slunk past me. We made eye contact for the briefest of moments, but he kept moving. We didn't like to acknowledge each other in public, but he knew what I was and I knew what he was.

I was a witch.

He was a vampire.

He'd sit in a different train car from me.

I pressed my forehead against the glass once more, unable to believe that I was doing the one thing I had promised myself I would never do: return to Shimmerfield.

Of course, that promise had been made before I'd gotten fired nine times in fourteen months after graduating from college.

But who was counting?

As easy as waving my hand, I was going home.

I'd need more than a spell to save me now.

Chapter Two

The train was taking me to Shimmerfield, the village on the coast of Maine where I had grown up. I had nowhere else to turn and I was desperate, so I was on my way.

The town of Shimmerfield was nice and quaint as only a small town could be. For that matter, the entire Maine coast was nice and quaint—and beautiful, and for the most part, empty.

Which was why Maine was the perfect place for supernatural creatures to live.

When I moved to the Big Apple after college, I thought I was starting with so much potential. Sure, I missed Haunted Bluff Mansion, but I had the world at my feet, and I was positive I'd never have to go back. What I had kept hidden, even from myself, was the certain knowledge in my heart of hearts that this day would come.

And now it had. I was on a train heading back to Maine and Haunted Bluff Mansion, which my family owned, operated, and lived in.

My family seat was a year-round haunted house.

All the supernaturals who worked there scaring the paying guests were real, inhabiting a house that my great-grandfather had started with my great-grandmother. They had come up with the idea in response to the fact that there were all sorts of supernatural creatures, from ghosts and ghouls to bats and the odd flying monkey, that would get out of hand if they didn't have something to do. The most requested supernaturals in the eyes of our customers were the skeletons, but le-haunts and ghosts followed closely behind.

My great-grandfather wanted to gainfully employ all these troublesome types, and so he did, working with the talents they already had. Once ghosts, skeletons, vampires, and le-haunts had their occupations in the haunted house to keep them out of trouble, it was much better for everyone. As one skeleton said proudly, "I don't even have to dress up for work now."

The ghosts particularly enjoyed their role, because they got to scare the humans and then fade into the background of the haunted mansion instead of being chased around with a broom they way ghosts usually have to work when they haunt someone. They're likely to get yelled at either way, but they don't mind that so much.

Before my great-grandparents started the mansion, supernaturals had started acting out and causing problems. Ghosts would jump out at people when they weren't supposed to. Vampires would stand outside people's homes and look terrifying. For a while, witch families didn't know what to do about the growing problem, but a solution soon became clear. For minor offenses, such as when a ghost decided to throw muffins and overturn tables, a stint at Haunted Bluff was in order. For major offenses, well, we weren't to talk about that. Over time, the mansion my great-grandfather had envisioned became less of a haven and more of a halfway house for difficult creatures of the afterlife persuasion.

We were open year-round, of course, since people were always up for a good scare.

Lucky for us, because it kept the ghosts entertained and out of any real trouble.

The mansion was gradually built up into an epic property, one where the magical world and the humans out for a spooky Friday night collided. We've chugged along for the last hundred years, and if you could ask my great-grandfather, what's even better than our longevity is that so many people connected to the place have died that we now have a real live graveyard out front, which totally adds to the haunted house ambiance!

My great-grandmother insisted that the graveyard be situated around the entrance gates, so everyone could see it and appreciate it as part of Haunted Bluff. Just because it wasn't visible from the house didn't mean my great-grandfather wasn't excited about it. When I was ten he took me out to the family plot and showed me where I'd be buried. I cried for a week.

Yup, that's my family.

Growing up at Haunted Bluff was no picnic. For one thing, a bunch of antiquated gender rules supposedly from times gone by were still alive and well in the witch community. As a witch, I hadn't gotten to do most of the fun stuff. Mostly the men went out and hunted for supernaturals, especially the law-breaking ones, an activity we called haunt hunting. The witches stayed at home and tended to the mansion, not that you were any slouch if you were capable of doing that.

There were the ghosts and the ghouls and of course the skeletons. Mostly they got along in harmony, but not all the time. When they argued, there was usually destruction of property involved (ours, not theirs), so I became adept at breaking up ghost fights. I had the unusual ability of being able to touch a ghost, which was very rare even in the witching world.

Hoping to retain at least a shred of my dignity, I hadn't told my family I was coming home. Even so, when my taxi drove up to the house I wasn't surprised to see my grandmother Cookie out front in a full black witch's costume–which witches don't actually wear–standing in front of a massive cauldron–which witches don't actually use–stirring slowly.

When I saw the old burn splotches on her clothes, I found myself rubbing at the angry bump on my face. Skin issues always mirrored my mood.

Cookie thought her antics added to the ambiance for visitors, but the rest of us knew the truth. She was hoping she could scare off anyone and everyone who came near the place.

Oftentimes, it worked. If you had to talk to Grandma Cookie, you'd be scared too.

I was breaking a rule by bringing a regular taxicab onto the property during the day (humans were allowed on the property only during business hours), but given how much stuff I had brought, there really was no choice.

Cookie took one look at me and her eyes went huge. She dropped her broom into the cauldron, turned around, and sprinted toward the house, long black skirts flapping.

Whoever said she was getting frail had definitely been lying.

"I hope she's happier to see you than she looks," said the cab driver in confusion.

"That's about how she always reacts when she sees me," I said.

The cab driver started to cluck with sympathy until I added, "And she's not the only one."

I raised my eyebrows at him in the mirror and he stopped chuckling. The fact that it was true didn't give him a right to point it out.

Suddenly, realizing that he was in a very strange place all by himself, with a girl whose trunk extolled the virtues of vampires, he clamped his mouth shut and stopped the car abruptly. Then he hopped out as quickly as he could, hustled around to open the trunk, and fetched my suitcases, placing them reverently on the loose stones of the driveway.

As he took in the imposing mansion, his mouth fell open. To his credit, the house was special enough to inspire that reaction.

Old black stone soared up five stories, fashioned into towers and framing broken windows and creepy-looking black ones. (The rooms with the broken windows were just for setting the mood. You had to use one only if you were in trouble with the powers that be, i.e., my grandmother.) The right color curtains did wonders to intensify the effect.

The cabby had already driven past the black iron gates, complete with the statues of two watchful cats, with some bats and skeletons thrown in for good measure. To top it all off there was a spire in the middle of the house with a giant cat on it: the family symbol. My great-grandfather had made it up because he thought it made him seem more official.

The cumulative effect finally got to the cabdriver. "This is quite the place," he said. "What did you say your family did here?"

"It's a year-round haunted house." I fired off the standard line I used with anyone who actually knew where I lived. At dinner parties in New York, you'd better believe I lied about my family's occupation!

The man nodded, but he still looked skeptical.

"It's very authentic-looking," he murmured, tipping his cap.

"We do try. You should come and check it out sometime," I added dryly as I hefted my bags and started moving away from him.

He bobbed his head in the way people do when they want to seem agreeable but are never really going to do what you're suggesting.

Not that I blamed him. I myself had tried to escape this place, and look where that had gotten me.

"Thanks for the help with the bags," I smiled.

The man swallowed hard and then, in an almost shaking voice, he said, "Want me to help you carry them in?"

"I can handle it," I said.

The instant relief on his face was typical. He told me to have a good day and nearly sprinted back to his car.

Dusk was falling, and the cab driver certainly couldn't be blamed for not wanting to be in the vicinity of Haunted Bluff Mansion when night came. I let him go without further ado, gathered my courage, and turned to face the house.

At that exact moment, three rotting eggs exploded on the ground next to my feet. I was under attack!

I gasped and ducked, then leapt out of the way and dashed for the big front door as fast as I could, dragging my luggage behind me. Eggs continued to explode, just missing me and my stuff every time.

Once I had gotten to the safety of the doorway, I glanced up and yelled, "GUS! STOP! NOW!"

Floating above me was a fat ghost, looking very pleased with himself. "You don't like the welcome?" he pouted.

"No throwing eggs at the family," I huffed. "Don't you remember the rules?"

Gus only looked more petulant. "You've been gone a long time! What do you know about the rules now? Maybe they've changed."

"Have they?" I challenged.

I tried the door, but it was locked, even though my grandmother Cookie had just run through it.

If it wasn't one thing it was another.

I pounded on the door and then pounded some more, while Gus grumbled something about picky Garbo women and floated away.

"That self-righteous cloud must be comfortable," I yelled after him.

He waved.

Fall was arriving, and the air was cold. Fighting to get my breath under control, I glared after Gus until he was out of view. Then I started worrying about how mussed my brown hair probably was. Not the greatest state in which to come crawling home to the family business.

While I waited for someone to let me in, I gazed around to see how they were keeping the place. Random hay bales dotted the yard, interspersed with crinkling old leaves and unkempt grass. There was something oddly charming about the mansion, and I had always liked the fact that people came here to spend their precious weekend evenings. It was fun, much more so since they didn't know it was real. And how they did appreciate our efforts at authenticity!

When I was almost tired of pounding, the thick wooden door finally flew backwards, almost knocking me off balance. I had to stop my hand in mid-swing lest I punch my grandmother.

"What do you want?" Cookie demanded as if she didn't even know who I was.

Thank goodness I'd avoided inheriting the nose, but it suited her well, like when she wanted to turn it up at people.

At the moment she was using her wide body to block my entrance.

"Hi Gram, nice to see you, too," I said, scrutinizing her and concluding that nothing much had changed since the last time I'd seen her. She was as short and squat as ever, with flyaway gray hair, a large nose, and an overgrown propensity for making life difficult.

I was hot and sweaty and I desperately wanted to get to my room, my one haven in the house, to lie down. After years of work I'd gotten my room just the way I wanted it, and it was the only thing that had made the thought of coming home bearable.

"Whatever. You said you were never coming back here," Cookie said, glaring at me from under the wide brim of her witch's hat. "You in trouble? Ran out on your rent? Can't blame me for believing your lies."

"I wouldn't do that," I said. "Anyhow, you told me you'd stop stealing spoons, but I see you haven't done it," I said, pointing to one of her bulging pockets.

"They're coins," she said, never looking away from me. "Don't come home and be nosy!"

"Sure they are," I shot back. She was still physically blocking the door, and I was itching to get inside before Gus came back with any more bright ideas.

"What's the magic word?" said Cookie.

"Move?" I offered.

She shook her head, a sly smile creeping across her old lips.

"Now?" I tried again.

"WRONG!" she cried gleefully.

The sun was setting and I was starting to feel cold in the gloom. I thought I might finally get into my own house when Cookie's milky blue eyes, ceaselessly roving behind me, caught sight of something that interested her.

"What's that?" She pointed and I looked over my shoulder, realizing my mistake too late as she slammed the door in my face.

I stood there for several seconds, wondering if the watching ghosts could see the steam coming out of my ears. Then I pounded on the door some more, and waited.

The next instant, the door was opened by a familiar and less crazy face.

"Hi, Mom," I said, trying not to sound desperate.

"Cookie said there was a homeless person on the stoop. I guess for once she didn't lie," said my mother, eyeing me up and down.

Cookie was my dad's mom, so my mom didn't look anything like her. Mom was taller, and she still had black hair and dark brown eyes that could pin you to the wall with a look, as my younger brother could tell you in detail. Cam had been having a lot of experience with that look during his teenage years, i.e., recently.

"Good to see you." She sounded measured, but she stepped aside all the same.

I was home.

Chapter Three

Once I was inside, Mom did give me a hug, which for her was the equivalent of throwing a party. Maybe Cookie's plan all along had been to make me feel lucky for getting to enter the house at all.

"You too," I said.

Then Mom reached down and hauled in my second trunk. Mercifully, I'd bought this one secondhand from a human, so all it had on it was a peace sticker.

As she maneuvered the luggage, I examined the sweeping interior of my family home and decided that nothing much had changed from when I'd last been there.

"You have a lot of stuff. More than you bring at Christmas. Planning to stay for a while?"

I told her I was.

"Good," was all she said.

"Place looks good," I observed.

"Mostly looks the same," Mom shrugged.

She kept the place running like clockwork, and unlike most of the rest of us, she always dressed in serious clothing. She was too busy worrying about entertaining the paying customers to dress up like Cookie.

"Luckily Cookie worries about that," she had commented once, "and not much else."

The black marble floor was scuffed and darkened by a thin layer of dust; it hadn't been mopped in years. If I craned my neck far enough backwards I could just see the chandelier high above my head.

The silver desperately needed a shining and had also turned black. The cobwebs were so thick I imagined ghosts took delight in hiding precious little odds and ends in the strong webs they'd stolen.

The sweeping staircase stood out in front of me. To its right was the ghosts' section of the haunted house; to the left, the bats' and skeletons'.

My mother led the way up the staircase, but instead of turning right or left, she pushed on the wall in front of us. It looked like the rest of the wall, but a door had been carved out of the wood. If you hit the right spot, it would swing inwards.

The family inhabited the third, fourth, and fifth floors, while the haunted house started on the second floor and you worked your way down.

The second staircase we now walked up was worlds away from the grand staircase of the entrance hall. It was practical, with uncarpeted wooden steps. On either side of it hung family portraits, charms, and other bits of decorations the family had acquired over the years. My mother insisted that we not have anything too nice in the family areas, because of what had happened to her favorite grandfather's clock many years ago. The short story was that it involved an overconfident cat and a very angry Cookie with a broom.

The family also used the back wing of the house, which was good some of the time but sometimes awkward. A handful of incidents had occurred over the years where very determined guests had come barging into the kitchen or the library looking for the exit. Some were particularly afraid of the ghosts or vampires in the haunted house, while others were just curious about the famous Garbo family that lived there. Locally famous, mind you; I never gave in to praise, but our house was quite the well known oddity around town.

My mom led me up to the fourth floor, where the bedrooms were, but when I started to turn off toward mine, she kept climbing.

"Um?" I demanded, stopping on the landing instead of following her further upstairs.

Standing outside the door to the family's living room, I could hear voices coming from inside it.

"My room is on the fourth floor, remember?" I asked.

Mom's face paled a little, not a good sign.

My mom was brazen; she had stood up to all sorts of supernaturals over the years. But to deal with her own children was another matter entirely.

"What did you do to my room?" I breathed.

"You weren't here," Mom fumbled, her face going from pale to bright red. "Had to move to the big city, you did. You can't expect that room to stay empty forever!"

Without another word I burst through the door and into the living room. Three pairs of eyes turned to look at me, and then my cousin Pep, who was just my age, uttered a cry and flung her arms around my neck. I wrapped my arms around her shoulders and we both cried into each other's hair.

"Girls are so confusing," came a guy's voice from behind Pep. I rolled my eyes, even though no one could see them because they were buried in Pep's hair.

The voice was that of my brother Cam, who was standing behind Pep. Next to him were Kip and Corey Woodson.

Kip and Corey were brothers and friends of the Garbo family. They had been raised by their father after their mother left, and then, when their father died, they'd come to live and help out at the mansion, since both my aunt Meg's husband and my dad were also gone. Kip was the talent and strength behind haunt hunting. He was very capable and showed it every day. Corey was also capable, but he preferred labs and experiments to real fighting.

What had happened was that back when my brother was a baby, there had been an entire group of haunt hunters: my dad and Meg's husband (two of Cookie's sons), and Kip and Corey's father, among others. They had been ambushed by a particularly nasty set of vampires and none of them had survived. Corey and Kip had already lost their mother, so we took them in at Haunted Bluff. They might not be blood family, but they were family just the same.

Cam was forever trying to keep up with them, and usually failing. We all babied him, but don't tell him I said that.

"Probably why you're still single." Kip reached out to ruffle Cam's hair, but Cam swatted his hand away.

"Jane, good to see you!" Corey came forward and wrapped his arms around both Pep and me. "Glad you're back!"

"Get off, you big lug," Pep choked out. "I can't breathe."

"Sounds like you can breathe just fine," said Corey, grinning broadly and stepping back to survey us.

Cam came over and gave me a hug, but he also whispered so no one else could hear the question: "Why did you come back? You got out!"

I pulled away and glared up at him. He got taller every time I saw him, and I wondered when he was going to stop.

"Don't make me regret my decision," I teased.

For a split second I thought Cam's face clouded, and I wondered why. But he recovered quickly, so I filed the question away for the time being.

"You headed to your room?" asked Kip, the quietest of the crew.

At that, all four young people exchanged concerned looks, then looked past me to my mom, who cleared her throat and shifted uncomfortably.

"She didn't tell you?" Pep squealed.

"Didn't tell me what?" I demanded.

This was bad, I knew it was going to be bad. Anything that inspired Kip to say a full and complete sentence was definitely worth worrying about.

Without another word I brushed past my cousins and hurried down the hall. I dropped my bags halfway, because I had a feeling I'd be taking them somewhere else pretty soon. I could hear the sound of feet hurrying after me, and maybe even a call for me not to be unreasonable, but I ignored all that.

What had she done with the place? I wondered. Turned it into a sewing room? No one in my family sewed . . .

A happy sigh of relief escaped me as I saw my doorway, light streaming through it as though welcoming me.

But when I stepped around the corner, I gasped in horror.

The room was perfectly neat. A bed with a blue bedspread was pushed into a corner, and a desk devoid of paper and writing implements sat near it. The rug had been removed and the window curtains had been changed from rebellious to boring.

"What is this?" I barely managed to get out. My bedspread had been a quilt that had been in the family for generations, I had a well-worn antique rug of the brightest blue, and you better believe my curtains were filled with pizzazz!

There was a long pause.

"Don't be upset," said my mother, almost sounding desperate. "We gave your room to Lizzie."

I choked. I had expected it was going to be bad, *known* it was going to be bad, but how could it truly be that bad?

Lizzie was another one of my cousins. She hadn't lived at the mansion growing up, unlike Pep and her sister Lark, but she'd always been nearby. I had always been able to feel her presence, like a leech. She was a year younger than I was, and unlike me, an exemplary witch. She did everything properly and as she was supposed to. Oh, and she was blonde and blue-eyed and pretty.

I couldn't stand her.

"You gave my room to Lizzie?" I breathed, so shocked I was unable to move.

"She needed to come here for training. You knew that day would come. She's learning with flying colors. That girl really is a marvel."

Lizzie's parents were modern types. They didn't care about their only child and spent their lives traveling. That was why they had given Lizzie permission to become a haunt hunter: no respect for tradition. No matter how much I wanted to hate them, there were times when I thought their behavior proved that they were the sanest of the lot.

I choked again. Pretty soon my mother would rush me to the hospital, except that she wouldn't, because she thought I was being too dramatic.

In my opinion, there was no such thing as too dramatic where Lizzie was concerned. The biggest dose of skepticism was the most accurate in any matter whatsoever that applied to Lizzie.

Just as my mom put her arm around my shoulder and led me away from my former beautiful room, the fourth floor door burst open and Grandma Cookie came storming in.

"Seen it already has she? Did she make a fool of herself? You should have waited for me," said Cookie gleefully.

"She's handling it just fine," Pep said. I gave her a swift glance to thank her for defending me.

"I'm never going to be the same again," I moaned, sinking down into a nearby chair. "Everything is lost!"

"Yeah, see, she's fine," said Pep.

"Where's she going to stay now?" Pep asked, looking concerned. "She could bunk with Lark and me, but it's already a tight squeeze."

"Absolutely not," I said. "You and Lark don't have enough room as it is, and anyhow I'd get in the way of all the black Lark puts everywhere. This place is big enough, you'd think we had enough bedrooms."

Lark liked black clothing, black decorations, and black possessions of all sorts. She felt that anything black was more real than anything else of any color whatsoever.

"There are the guest bedrooms," I said brightly. I had never once been allowed to stay in the nice rooms set aside for guests, but I had never really cared, because I until now I'd had my own beloved room. But the guest rooms were by far the best rooms in the house, and I was already starting to feel a little intrigued about them. They had views of the cliff and the ocean, which family members didn't have in their own rooms because my mom didn't have any use for time wasters like ocean-gazing when there was so much work to be done.

"You'll have to kick Lady Oakley out of the attic. That's the only option," said my mom.

I groaned loudly. The punishments were adding up.

"Pep, will you help Jane get set up in the attic? Lark should be back soon, and she can help too."

I brightened a little bit at the prospect of seeing Lark, younger than Pep by a year. The poor girl had to share a birthday with Lizzie, but that's where their similarities ended. She was one of my favorites in the family, and we had always been close.

Lark and Pep might share the same parents, but that was about all they had in common. Where Lark was sarcastic, Pep was serious. Where Pep thought that success at test-taking was the secret to a happy life, Lark burned her assignments in front of teachers. Unlike her sister, Lark was slower and more methodical most of the time, while Pep pinged around life as if she were forever being shot from one cannon to the next. Still, they loved each other with an unbreakable bond.

Lark had the brightest, reddest, curliest hair I'd ever seen. Her strands escaped hair ties so often they'd have made exceptional career criminals. Usually, she did a fishtail braid slung over one shoulder to keep her hair under control. She also liked to dye one streak of hair bright white. Her mother told her she looked like a Santa Claus skunk, but Lark thought it made her stand out.

As if she needed a white streak to accomplish that.

She had a nose ring to go with her black clothes, another point of contention with her mother Meg, who was more traditional. But at least Aunt Meg had Pep, who wouldn't dream of coloring her hair or wearing all black clothing.

All of this was despite the fact that Meg herself had colored her hair every shade of blue, pink, purple, and red under the sun. Meg had been the wild child growing up, but she had settled into a woman who liked pretty things and liked her independence, thank you very much.

I had always thought Pep would be more at home at a private school, where she might actually have thrived. Instead she was fated to run a haunted house gift shop. Ours was called Enchanted Bits and Bobs, Odds and Ends, BOO.

"Come on!" said Pep, taking me by the arm and leading me away from the carnage.

We climbed to the fifth floor in silence, giving in to my final humiliation. I had been relegated to the attic, and not just any attic: this was crazy Lady Oakley's attic.

"Just ignore her," Pep said. "She's harmless."

I knew she was just trying to encourage me, but I was having a hard time buying it. "If she's so harmless, why are you whispering?" I wondered.

Pep shrugged, her face reddening. "She's never hurt anyone."

"She just wants us to think that," I added darkly. "She's lulling us into a false sense of calm, and when she has us completely fooled, that's when she'll strike."

"That's the spirit," said Pep sarcastically. Then she swung the attic door open and said, "Here we are."

To be fair, the house had three attics. We were currently standing in the one to the right of the stairs, otherwise known as my new room. There was another to the left and another in a separate part of the house where my family stored endless amounts of stuff, so much stuff, in fact, that we could have turned the place into a store and not run out of things to sell for years.

"Where's my bed?" I asked, looking around.

At the opposite end of the space was a small, grimy window, and between there and where we were standing, looking in through the door, the only thing I could see was dust.

In case I'm not making it totally clear, the attic that my mother had just given me for my bedroom was empty except for the dust piled in the corners and filtering gently through the air, disturbed by the opening of a door that until a few moments ago probably hadn't been opened in months.

"Left side," said Pep, thumbing over her shoulder. "We'll get everything settled."

We dropped my suitcases on the old floorboards and turned our attention to getting the furniture out of the other room and set up in my new space. If this was going to be home from now on, I was most definitely going to make it as comfortable as rickety attic furniture would allow.

Getting a few things out of storage, however, was easier said than done. The dust had become quite possessive of the side table and wanted to hang onto it. I won in the end, but not until I'd spent a solid minute coughing.

"This might not be so bad," I said at last, patting the bed, where I'd sat down to take a break. I took a bit of consolation from the fact that at least the mattress seemed to be relatively new.

Further advantages had occurred to me as Pep and I moved things around. There was a lot of space up here, and I was so far away from the other rooms in the house that it would also be fairly quiet. Haunted Bluff was rarely quiet, especially when Cam, Kip, and Corey got going (boys will be boys, you know), but not even they ventured up here very often.

I wasn't going to admit it out loud, but maybe Lizzie had actually done me a favor . . . ?

I quickly banished the thought; I actually wasn't going to admit it even to myself, let alone anyone else. Being even a little bit charitable toward Lizzie was just not within my power.

Chapter Four

Suddenly, there was thunder on the stairs.

Pep was about to say something when the door creaked open.

"You came back!"

A girl with an ear-to-ear grin and messy red hair piled haphazardly on top of her head shot into the attic. She was wearing ripped black jeans and a black sweater covered in sparkling ice cream cones.

"Nice outfit," I said.

"It's vintage, darling," she said, pausing briefly to pose.

After Lark and I gave each other a hug, we all settled in to get me feeling at home again. Pep sat on a box of books while Lark disappeared into the other attic and dragged out a rocking chair that groaned as she carried it.

"There's a lot of cool furniture up here," Lark commented with approval. "You're going to make this room sweet. We should take a couple of the pieces and paint them black for our room," she said, turning to Pep.

"No," said Pep.

Just then there was a series of thumps, and I glared at the wall. The plaster was so old I could see bits of it coming off with each thump.

"Cut it out, Lady Oakley," I yelled. The thumping stopped.

"Good thing she doesn't mind my being here," I muttered. " And don't try to make me feel better about Lizzie taking my room," I warned darkly. "I don't intend to forgive her."

"You might as well forgive her for that and stay mad at her about everything else," said Pep.

"What everything else?" I said.

"The last twenty-five years," said Pep.

"That goes without saying," I grumbled.

Lark had brought a sandwich with her, and it wasn't until I saw it that I realized how hungry I was myself.

"Anyhow, you're going to make this room your own," Pep said encouragingly. "We'll help, and it'll be great."

A sudden crash brought the three of us to our feet. This time I didn't think it was Lady Oakley; her revenge for my yelling at her would have been subtler. Lark sprang up so suddenly that her sandwich went flying everywhere. Looking around and not seeing anyone, she calmly started picking the pieces up off the floor and putting them back on her plate. But she kept an eye on the room while she did it, as if waiting to see whether whatever had caused the disturbance was going to show itself.

"What was that?" I demanded. The noise had sounded like it came from several floors down, but it had been so loud that I was afraid the house might collapse around us.

"The ghosts!" Pep exclaimed.

"Which ghosts?" I demanded. There were so many these days . . .

"The new ones! We've been having the worst time getting them settled," Pep said, shaking her head. "As usual, the old ghosts are laughing at us and not helping one bit. In fact, they're showing the new ones pranks and ways to get in trouble, which basically amount to lessons in how to make your mom mad."

"Typical stuff," said Lark, before taking another large bite of sandwich.

"We'd better get downstairs," said Pep, standing up and heading for the door, while Lark stuffed the rest of her pre-dinner snack into her mouth.

The three of us rushed down the four flights of stairs to the grand entrance hall, where we found pandemonium. The ghosts must have come in right after Mom took me upstairs, and they were causing havoc.

"I like how Cookie tried to keep me out of the house, but these goons are fine to let in," I muttered.

"No, this is MY lamp! It's not your lamp!" One ghost kept floating through a lamp on the side table (and the side table itself) and giggling uproariously.

"I could get used to this place," cackled another as he winged and zinged around the room at breakneck speed. "So many things to break and so little time!"

"Wheeeeee!!!!" a third one cried, flipping end over end in the air.

"Come down here! How dare you!" Aunt Meg was racing around with a broom, swinging it wildly in every direction. The ghosts merely scattered and laughed.

Aunt Meg was small, and Pep took after her in that way. Both daughters had their mom's curly hair, although Pep's was brown like her mother's, in contrast to Lark's blazing red curls.

Meg was nothing like my own mother. Meg loved to dress up and wear fancy clothing. She loved thrift shops more than anything else in the world and she never wore the same clothes twice. Today she was in silk pants that had a teal and light brown map of the world on them. She wore her gold shirt tucked in. Neither of her daughters was anywhere near as flashy as their mother. "There aren't enough clothes for more than one Meg," Lark had told me once.

"If you don't come down I'll perform an enchantment on you," cried a new voice from down the stairs.

I closed my eyes in consternation. When would Lizzie learn to butt out? The girl only lived here, it wasn't like she was really one of us, so it was really none of her business.

"Threatening ghosts never works," Lark said, just as annoyed as I was. "It just makes them more likely to dance on the table tops and throw things at us."

"What's the point of being good at salsa if we don't take advantage of it?" burst out a giggling ghost who had heard what Lark said. Then the ghost fell backwards laughing.

My redheaded cousin leaned forward, held her palm flat under her chin, and blew. The air that flew out of her mouth was sparkling white and flowed smoothly over the laughing ghost. Taken by surprise, the new recruit was pushed backwards, away from the table.

"They really are witches!" another ghost cried. "I wasn't sure I believed it! How very exciting!"

"Aren't you glad you came home?" Meg panted as she rushed past me. "Lark, you know you aren't supposed to use magic on the ghosts unless it's absolutely necessary."

"It was," Lark argued. "There was a ghost in front of me, so it was necessary."

"How do you figure?" Meg demanded.

"They were starting to really annoy me," said Lark.

"Leave the redhead alone! She doesn't have a sense of humor," cried a ghost with a double chain necklace.

"If only you'd say something funny," Lark said.

I turned to watch my pretty cousin Lizzie descending the stairs. She was wearing leather pants and a black leather blouse. As she took another step down the stairs, three ghosts darted toward her and overwhelmed her.

"Maybe this one will be more fun," cried the ghost woman who'd wanted to salsa.

"Trust me, she isn't," I murmured.

"Hey, we died! The least you can do is let us have these little amusements," cried another ghost as Meg unleashed a fresh round of fury.

Just then Lizzie cried out, ducking away as the new ghosts messed up her perfect hair and tugged on her ears. She tried to swing back at them, but she didn't have the same special ability I did, so it didn't do any good. Her next ploy was to cover her head with her arms and whimper in frustration.

"She should have learned the blowing trick," said Lark smugly.

"Help her," Aunt Meg demanded.

"You already told me not to use magic. I'm so confused," Lark shrugged.

Pep, Lark, and I turned to look at a flailing Lizzie, while Meg got even more frustrated.

"I'm talking to you, Jane," Meg glared at me, ignoring her daughter's backtalk.

"I think her hair looks good pulled on end," I offered.

My aunt gave me a look that would have boiled water and pointed an imperious finger at Lizzie. To be fair, she was also clearly trying not to laugh, so I rolled my eyes and without waiting another second marched forward toward the ghosts.

The one wearing chains was nearest, so I simply grabbed him by the shoulder and flung him backwards. Salsa ghost lady gasped, then turned to Lark, and said, "That was much more impressive than your blowing. I'm Glenda, by the way."

Ghosts weren't something I could hurt by touching them, and by the same token, flinging them across the room wasn't going to do them any damage. But I always felt better when I did it. To everything and everyone but me, they weren't solid beings but wisps of smoke and mist.

I looked at the chaos before me and shook my head in bemusement.

Just back from the big city as I was, it struck me forcefully that there was something about this mansion that wasn't serious. It was just a big stage for weekend fun and adventure, where people came to escape from their real lives. Everything here was authentic, but not necessarily real. There was an order and a way of doing things that had gone on for generations, and despite how every new ghost and le-haunt thought he or she could disrupt it, they always failed in the end.

And in the end, I finally moved over to help Lizzie. I'll be honest, I moved more slowly than I would have if they'd been harassing Pep, but once I got their attention, the three new ghosts assembled quietly. Despite their seeming surrender, however, they didn't quite understand what they were getting into.

I reached up and brushed my hand against the nearest ghost, pulling him away from Lizzie, who was whimpering and trying to put her hair back into place.

"Don't be difficult, George," Glenda advised. The ghost was so surprised that he went willingly. Then the other two turned to look at me, almost gleefully.

Here we go, I thought.

"You're one of the few," breathed George.

"Here, I'm one of the many," I corrected, not wanting them to think they could bother the rest of the Garbos.

"You leave her alone. Only her family gets to harass her," said Pep with a grin.

"You're like normal families," the chain ghost said dryly. "Fine, I'll be delighted to go where I'm supposed to." He sounded imperious as he waited for someone to show him the way, and my Aunt Meg was so relieved that they'd calmed down, she did just that.

Lizzie didn't waste any time being grateful to me, being too busy fixing her lipstick. She'd gotten her hair back in place except for one strand that was sticking straight up the back of her head. I had an internal debate about whether to tell her, but I decided she'd walk past a mirror soon enough.

In fact, I was surprised she hadn't magicked a mirror to trail along next to her at all times, preferably with camera lighting secured around the edges.

"Well, well, well, look who decided to come crawling back," she simpered at last.

Yup, no gratitude would be forthcoming. Lizzie only talked in simper, which didn't leave any room for saying "Thank you."

"Yeah, I missed the place and some of the people," I said.

She smirked. "That's not what I heard. What I heard was that you couldn't hold onto a real job so you had to come crawling back here to live with your mom."

"Isn't what we do here a real job?" I asked.

"I'm saying you don't think it is," she rolled her eyes.

"You could just say thank you," Pep pointed out to her blond cousin.

"I could've dealt with them," said Lizzie, blinking furiously. She did that when she was lying.

"You were doing a great job," said Lark.

"Sorry about your room, by the way. I decided to liven things up a bit," said Lizzie, quickly regaining her balance and simpering some more. How she thought navy curtains and no decorations on the walls livened anything up I'd never know, because I didn't care enough to find out.

"Don't even worry about it," I smiled brightly. "I'm very happy in the attic."

Before she could tell how badly I was lying, I turned and walked away.

Having gotten the ghost management episode out of the way, I wanted to get to the kitchen as soon as possible. I hadn't been home in months, and the kitchen was where all the wonderful things in the mansion happened.

Like cake.

Pep and Lark followed me, leaving Lizzie on the stairs to clean up the ghosts' mess by herself.

The hallways were wide, and usually dark, the mahogany paneling old but still beautiful. We had made it halfway down the hall when, without warning, the door to our right burst open and a skeleton shot out.

"Grrrrr," said the skeleton, holding up bones for hands in a scary manner.

"Hi, Steve. How are you?" I asked.

"Jane! Goodness, it's been a long time. Top of the morning to you! I'm well," His lips cracked and shifted into a skeleton version of a smile. Then he backed up and closed himself back in the closet.

Even if I hadn't known where the kitchen was, I could have found it by the wonderful smells that were now filling the hallway.

Aunt Audrey was always making something incredible.

Audrey, the only resident of Haunted Bluff I hadn't seen yet, was Cookie's other son's widow. Uncle Bill had died under mysterious circumstances when I was young, leaving behind a new wife and no children.

Given that Audrey knew we were all witches, she couldn't very well go back and have a normal life. Besides, she had grown very close to my mother and was happy to stay and lead a witch's life. Audrey, my mom, and Meg had been best friends for ages.

Audrey didn't like the ghosts and skeletons much, so she usually worked in the kitchen, creating gourmet meals for the rest of us.

I had barely set foot in the kitchen when a plate of cookies was shoved into my hands. With such good fortune, how was I to say no?

"It's so good to have you back," Audrey beamed at me.

I took a cookie, sat down at the big counter that dominated the center of the room, and thought about all the time I'd spent in this space.

The kitchen was the most sacred space in the house, and the one that we tried hardest to keep clear of any ghost groups or other nasty creatures. It just wasn't sanitary to have them hanging around.

What made the room even more inviting was that my aunt Audrey loved ambiance and color and had made the kitchen her own domain. I always loved hanging out there, and no, it wasn't just because of the cookies. Okay, it was a lot because of the cookies. But I also just liked the space, and felt happy there.

Aunt Audrey beamed at me.

"I trust the trip wasn't too awful?" she asked.

She went back to chopping carrots, but not before giving Lark a glare and asking, "Was the sandwich enough or do you need more?"

Lark went red. Clearly she hadn't thought Audrey would notice her taking a sandwich from the fridge.

"I might like another," said Lark, her blush deepening.

"Sure thing, you can make your own," Audrey said, pointing to the fridge.

At Haunted Bluff, everyone had a job to do. My mom kept everything running smoothly while Meg oversaw all the new ghostly additions, did a lot of the decorating, and made sure that our current residents were well cared for and not running around scaring the townsfolk willy-nilly.

Meg's daughters, my cousins, were in charge of helping Meg, but also of making sure the grounds kept their ambiance for the paying customers. It wasn't enough that this place actually *was* a haunted house. No one would believe a haunted house that didn't also *look* haunted. Luckily, Grandmother Cookie helped a lot with that effort just by being herself.

"How long are you going to stay this time?" my aunt asked.

I shrugged. I wasn't ready to say I'd moved back home for good, because in my heart of hearts I told myself I might get to leave again. In my even deeper heart I didn't believe I would, but I wasn't going to say that out loud.

At least not yet.

"A while," I said evasively.

"Good, you can help with what's going on here . . ." Lark didn't get a complete sentence out of her mouth before Pep delivered a sharp kick to her shins.

"Ouch," cried Lark. She glared, but she also stopped talking.

"What was that about?" I asked, looking amongst the three of them.

"Oh, nothing," said Audrey casually. "We're just really glad you're home. The SpookyBooSpectacular is coming up. It's going to be a grand time."

The three of them exchanged a significant look. Lark had most definitely not been talking about the big Spooky Event we had every year, but I knew I wasn't going to get anything out of them right now. If I wanted to know what was really going on I'd have to get Lark alone, and given the determined expression on her older sister's face and the fact that the Garbos didn't believe in alone time, that was going to be a challenge.

"Is there anything we can help you with right now? Chocolate chip cookie-making, perhaps?" Pep asked Audrey.

My plump aunt laughed. "Don't take me for a fool. I know you're supposed to be cleaning the bowls. I'll make cookies for you all later." The bowls were the large pots we used to collect money every weekend, and cleaning them was a chore.

Pep brightened. "I can get through anything with your cookies!"

"I'll make them faster with flattery," my aunt confirmed.

"Aren't you glad to be home?" Pep asked me, referring to the cookies. I nodded.

"Since you're glad, do you want the good news first or the bad news?" said Lark, turning to me.

"Give her the good news first," said Pep.

"Okay," said Lark. "The good news is that the haunted house is more popular than ever. We get great reviews all the time."

"Most of them reference how authentic the place is," said Pep. "Go figure."

"Shocking," I said, picking up another cookie and munching on it.

"We're doing really well," said Lark.

Just then there came a banging on the window. Without missing a beat, Audrey grabbed a cloth, turned around, and like a fabulous baseball player chucked the cloth at the window.

Annoyed, the skeleton turned away.

"What's the bad news?" I asked.

"You came home just in time for season opener," said Pep with a big grin.

I groaned.

Chapter Five

We were closed during August, but otherwise the haunted house ran year-round. It was open four days a week leading up to Halloween, and I had come home just in time for the season to get into full swing. In other words, we were up and running with a vengeance. This was no time of year to mess around.

From the time I was little I had hated going into the haunted house by myself, and I never did so if I could help it. This might sound silly coming from a real witch, especially because over the years the ghosts and skeletons had often taken pity on the silly little witch I'd been, but I couldn't help it. Haunted houses are scary!

"You'd think knowing that skeletons were real would make them less terrifying," mused Lark as she nibbled another sandwich. Like everyone else in the house, Lark knew I was never thrilled with the haunted house.

"I'm not scared of them. It's the darkness, the hay sticking out of the cracked walls, the echoes, and the spider webs that get me," I shivered.

"It's a good thing Kip and Corey like all that stuff so much," said Pep, "because I want nothing to do with it."

For the most part, the ghosts, vampires, le-haunts, and skeletons themselves kept the haunted house in tiptop shape. Whenever a customer was so afraid that he or she broke, smashed, or ruined something, usually someone fixed it before it became a big deal. Lark, Pep, and I found other ways to be useful around the Bluff, but at least we didn't have to do much in the haunted house.

Only thing was, we weren't allowed to go supernatural hunting. Yes, that's right. My family gathered the ghosts from houses they were haunting, cemeteries they were ruining, and anywhere else they might have gotten to, and told them we'd give them loads of people to haunt without their having to search them out at all. The Garbos went to cemeteries and told all the skeletons milling about that they had something better for them to do. There was the occasional trouble with a skeleton who was having a little too much fun preying on the living, but for the most part even the stubborn ones were fetched back to Haunted Bluff Mansion without much difficulty.

"Oh, did you hear about the flying ghost bats? That was funny." Pep keeled backwards giggling.

"They were attacking the back wing of the mansion, but they couldn't do any damage, because they're ghosts," Lark explained.

"They'd need someone to pour water on them," I mused.

Lark and Pep, who had busied themselves getting tableware out for dinner, went white. It was a little known fact that water solidified ghosts for a short period of time. For that reason, ghosts became all the more dangerous in the rain.

Most ghosts didn't know this about themselves (because it wasn't as if they'd been offered ghosts histories and life lessons while they were still living humans), and we tried to cycle ghosts in and out of the mansion relatively quickly so they couldn't chat with each other long enough to find out. A ghost uprising was my mother's biggest fear.

"The full moon makes it worse too," Pep pointed out. "That's another layer."

"Right, I forgot," I said. The haunted house was at its most dangerous during the full moon. Whenever the full moon was due, my mom would get into a dither about whether to close the house if rain was forecast. She was afraid the ghosts would become unmanageably rambunctious if given that golden opportunity.

"Anyway, live bats saw the ghost bats and got very upset," laughed Lark. "They were flying through the air one minute and flying into ghosts the next."

I shook my head. "The poor bats."

"How about you three help me make dinner?" Audrey broke in suddenly. "You can save your chores and work on them tomorrow."

We were all happy enough to drop the chores for today and help Audrey make a delicious meal.

It took a lot to keep the family business up and running, and we all had a lot to do at the best of times. Kip, Corey, Cam, and Lizzie were around to help my mom and Meg run the place, and yes, I intentionally didn't include Cookie on that list, though she did help in her own fashion by pretending to brew her potion on the front lawn. A little known fact was that customers thought she was muttering potion ingredients as she stood out there stirring, but she was really muttering curses on the guests.

Luckily, the curses weren't real. At least as far as we knew.

"I have to work in the gift shop tonight, but I'll be at dinner for sure, at least for a little while," said Pep, who had taken over the Haunted Bluff gift shop from Cookie to the great relief of the family, the paying customers, and all future paying customers, because we actually needed to sell gift items and customers actually wanted to buy them. All Cookie had done for her past few years in the gift shop was to yell at happy couples and groups of excited friends who had arrived looking forward to an entertaining haunted house.

"She's much better as a front lawn decoration," I said of our grandmother.

"Yes, now when she does something offensive they think she's in character," sighed Pep. "It's a good disguise that way."

"They think she's just acting like a witch, when in reality . . ." I let that hang there until we all burst out laughing.

"How's Taft?" I asked.

My great-uncle had gone crazy a few years ago, announcing one day that he believed there was a conspiracy among the vampires for world domination. He kept warning us of that fact, saying it was only a matter of time. He would run around the house changing all the clocks and having sword fights with the air, apparently preparing for the great final battle.

"He's the same," said Pep carefully. "He's around here somewhere, though he doesn't show himself as often as he used to. Mom was worried about him for a while, but she's gotten over it. He's made great friends with all the new ghosts and they watch out for him when they can. Even the skeletons seem to like him. Cookie tried to help him get lost and never return, but he found his way back. Now Cookie's banned from 'helping' any of us."

I shook my head. There were no words. "I wish the skeletons would warm to Cookie like they've warmed to Uncle Taft."

"Cookie is lacking a witchy warmth, a . . . basic humanity, shall we say . . . that Uncle Taft is not," Pep observed.

"I suppose Cookie wouldn't be Cookie if she weren't causing trouble," I said.

"You could say that for anyone in the family," said Lark with a grin. "It's a wonder we hold this place together."

"Anything else been going on?" I wondered.

Lark and Pep both fell silent again. In fact, their guilty faces had returned, while Audrey scrubbed ever harder at the sweet potatoes. I knew very well that they were holding something back, but I couldn't figure out what could be so bad that they wouldn't just tell me.

"Everything is good! We're glad you're back," said Pep brightly.

"Yeah, well, I tried not to come back. I got fired from a lot of jobs. I would have preferred to keep working at the law office to coming back here, so you can see how desperate I was to stay away. But even those crooks fired me in the end."

"We understand that you didn't necessarily want to embrace the whole haunted house thing again, but you're here now, and I'm sure you're going to make the best of it," said Lark. "And anyhow, I'm so glad to have you back!"

"You could get a nose ring. I bet that would make you feel better," said Pep.

"You're only saying that because your mom and mine would be mortified," I said.

"Yes, their mortification is why you should feel better," grinned Pep. "It certainly helped me."

All this talk of welcoming me home reminded me that something was missing, and suddenly I realized what it was.

"Where's Rose, anyway?" I asked.

Rose was the best cat in the history of best cats. She was snow white with bright blue eyes and a bushy and judgmental tail.

"Probably out killing something," said Lark. "Hopefully mice. We've had to talk to her about the mice, actually. We need some left alive for the sake of haunted house authenticity, but she seems determined to kill every single one single-paw-edly. I think she's laughing at your mom's declaration that if we only have one cat, some of the mice will survive."

"She's not eating all of them, either. No, sometimes she's just bored," said Pep, shaking her head. "It's not really sanitary."

"Cats are plenty sanitary and Rose is the best." I decided there and then to go find her before dinner and say hi.

Ghosts are a more supernatural white than the cat, but ever since we'd gotten Rose, some of them had mistaken her for one of them and tried to get her to do things she couldn't, like fly or go through walls. In the end she just yelled at them, explaining that her white fur was real, whereas nothing about a ghost was real, and if they didn't stop it she'd get really mad.

No one wanted to see Rose mad, though the mice no doubt minded more than the ghosts.

"Remember when you first got Rose?" Lark said.

I rolled my eyes. "It took so much to convince Mom to get a cat." Rose had showed up as a stray, and Mom didn't want to keep her. "She was worried about the fact that Rose was white, but black would have been worse. Black cats spell doom, at least people think so."

"But a white cat does look spooky darting across the fields at night. It really is like she's a ghost," Lark shivered. "I wish I could be a ghost and scare people."

"Rose would probably say she doesn't need to be a ghost to scare people," Pep said.

"That's one of the good things about coming back," I said. "There was no room for me to have a cat in New York. Now I have Rose again."

At that point the conversation was diverted by the fact that dinner was ready.

It was time to face the music: the whole family together.

Chapter Six

Dinner with all the family present could only be described as stress-inducing. Historically I had tried to avoid it by eating early, eating late, or not eating at all. Anything, really, to skip out on Cookie's orders and my mother spinning on about work.

My sneaky mother had taken the opportunity of my return to the Bluff to insist that we all have a celebratory meal. Lark, Pep, and I thought it was unnecessary punishment on top of the simple fact of my return, but it really wasn't avoidable.

At least Audrey's delicious food was some compensation.

At dinner that night were my grandmother Cookie, my great-uncle Taft, Kip and Corey, and my younger brother, not to mention my mom and my two aunts. Lizzie, Lark, Pep and I rounded out the gathering.

When I greeted Uncle Taft, he peered at me and asked if I was from the 1920s or the 1930s. I told him I was from a totally different century, and that really blew his mind. He was in an old white and red dress uniform, complete with an eyeglass and a sword hanging at his side.

"How are the ghosts settling in, Meg?" Lizzie asked immediately.

Lark and Pep could barely contain their annoyance.

Meg loved to talk about work and Lizzie loved to ingratiate herself.

After a long day, Meg had changed into a red, flowing dress. Real fire danced along the hem. My mother hated that Meg used enchantments on her clothing. Meg did it more once she found that out.

"They're settling in nicely in one of the back fields," said Meg. "They really like the upper floor of the haunted house, so hopefully they can work up there until they're feeling more at home."

"And how is your work going?" Lizzie turned to Pep.

Pep enjoyed running the gift shop, and business had been great since she took over. She was born to work with customers and she was great at selling. Still, we'd had an issue recently with a skeleton getting loose and smashing up some of the glass trinkets in the store, and Pep had had to spend a week cleaning up and doing inventory, with all her other work delayed in the meantime. I could see all these thoughts and one more, pure annoyance, flash across her face and disappear in the span of a second.

"It's going well. I think sales will be brisk this weekend," she said in a stubborn monotone.

This weekend was known as the soft opening, while next weekend was the extravaganza known as the SpookyBooSpectacular. We had a long tradition of offering a quiet opening weekend to get all the kinks worked out. Then we really kicked things up a notch the following weekend. Now that the haunted house was so well known, there was a lot of pressure to make the big weekend spectacular.

"Of course they will be," Lizzie smirked.

"What will you be doing this weekend?" I asked her.

Pep gave me a grateful look. I thought it was a perfectly innocent question, but apparently it wasn't. The entire table fell silent, including Lizzie, who loved any opportunity to make me feel inferior.

After a beat of silence, Lizzie brushed off my question entirely, intent on making a show of leaving me in suspense. "Oh, you know. The usual."

"No, I don't know the usual, because I haven't been living here," I replied. "Which is why you took my room."

I saw my mother's eyes close in rising consternation, but I didn't care.

Lizzie's expression now changed to one of delight. She had been looking to me for a sign that I was upset about the room, and now I had given it to her. Silently cursing myself, I waited for her response. "It's just such a nice room," she said yet again.

"Have you heard any strange sounds?" Lark asked.

"In my room?" Lizzie asked, her face paling.

"Maybe, I can't really remember where I heard them." Lark tapped her mouth, pretending to think. "But it was most definitely when I was passing Jane's old door."

"I've heard funny sounds too, but this is a haunted house," her mother chided her. "I'm sure it's nothing."

We all ate in silence for a few minutes, then Cookie said sarcastically, "I'm so glad we could all get together as a family."

"Would you rather be eating alone?" I asked.

"Yes," she said.

"You're welcome to leave," Lark offered.

"My daughters-in-law made me come," she grumbled. "Besides, I'm old. If anyone's going to leave it's going to be the rest of you."

"Where should we have dinner, if not right here?" I asked.

"Maybe one of the barns," said Cookie after a moment of thought. "That's far away."

I leaned over to Lark and whispered, "Have they improved since I left?"

"I wouldn't say so, no," she replied.

"What are you nattering on about?" Uncle Taft demanded.

Whenever he talked he yelled, because he couldn't hear. When we told him we could hear just fine, so he didn't need to holler, he didn't remember five minutes later, so he yelled again. Grandmother Cookie had no tolerance for the man. To be fair, she hadn't had any tolerance for him when they were younger, either.

"It don't matter and stop yelling," chided Cookie.

"I never yell," yelled Uncle Taft.

I massaged my temples with my hands and looked down at my food, hoping it would save me.

"This salad is delicious," said Cam.

"That explains why you're eating all of it," said my mom.

"This is just my third helping. I'm a growing boy. I still don't eat as much as Corey," Cam protested.

"You're trying to eat us out of house and home," laughed Meg.

"I have to keep my strength up for . . ." He winced and yelped, "Ouch!" Then he glared at Kip, who had just kicked him under the table.

Again there was silence, and again I felt like somebody wasn't saying something they should have been saying, from my point of view.

So I decided it was time to press the point.

"What do you need your strength for?" I asked.

My brother coughed, a sure sign that he was lying, and said, "Usual rough-and-tumble stuff of the weekend. The ghosts are an awfully active lot recently."

"Right, I believe you. Not," I said, staring hard at my younger sibling.

"Healthy dose of skepticism is the only way to go into conversations with this family," Cookie sniffed.

"What do you know? You lie about tying your shoes in the morning," my mother scoffed.

"Are you saying I can tie my shoes and I'm just lying to get somebody else to do it?" Cookie asked.

The entire table chorused, "Yes."

"Aren't family dinners great?" Audrey asked.

Cookie reached over and put a comforting hand on her arm, "Get out while you can."

Audrey threw back her head and laughed.

"We'll have to work extra hard this weekend. Saturday is a full moon, after all," my mother cautioned, getting down to business.

It was Thursday, so that left us with just that night and the next day to do the hard work we were responsible for. Even worse, the ghosts and the skeletons, not to mention the bats, were more rambunctious during full moons, and I wasn't looking forward to the potential problems.

We had just moved on from the delicious lasagna to dessert, which was either chocolate lava cake, tiramisu, or strawberry shortcake, or if you were my little brother, all three, when the lights flickered.

"Man the battlements. Bring up your defenses. Destruction is coming," my great-uncle yelled, holding aloft an imaginary sword and staring straight ahead as he recited his battle cry.

"I'll be right back," said Corey. He dropped his napkin and got up from the table, taking his tiramisu with him as he went to look into the disturbance.

"It's probably nothing," Meg said, but she looked nervous.

"Why aren't more of us fighting?" Uncle Taft demanded. Then he seemed to forget about it and sat back down to tackle his dessert.

"I don't know what dinner you've been at, but we've been fighting all night," said Lark.

"Excellent," said Uncle Taft.

"If Corey doesn't come back with anything, do I have your permission to investigate the disturbance myself?" Lizzie asked my mother.

"No, I'm sure Corey will look thoroughly, and there probably won't be anything there," my mom said.

It didn't take long for Corey to return. "I didn't see anything," he said neutrally. Then he sat back down and set the empty tiramisu plate on the table.

"You have to try the strawberry shortcake. It's the best," said my brother.

"I made it," said Lark dryly.

"Okay, so the best is a stretch," said Cam.

"Does that mean you aren't going to eat it?"

"Second best is still pretty good," he replied, tucking in.

"Goodness this is boring," complained Cookie.

"Can you think of a better topic?" I asked my grandmother.

"You could tell us about New York. What made you leave?" she asked.

My face went instantly red; I should have known she'd go there. I was upset enough about being fired from so many jobs, and having to come home, without having my nose rubbed in it.

"I lost a couple of jobs and thought maybe I should come back home to Bluff," was all I said.

"You mean you were fired?" Cookie demanded. Out of the corner of my eye I saw Lizzie smirking.

"You could say that," I admitted.

"Yes, that's why I just did," she said. "Don't worry. This is where you belong anyway. I'm sure they were silly for letting you go."

"That's the nicest thing you've ever said to me," I told her. I'd been bracing myself for something horrible, and instead she'd said something really sweet. I almost felt better.

"Don't get used to it."

Just then there was a smashing noise; it sounded as if a lot of wood had been hit hard, and splintered. The lights flickered again and we all shot to our feet in the middle of clattering silverware and the scraping of chairs.

"Cauldrons of witches' fire come forth," my grandmother started to chant. She closed her eyes and raised her hands as the lights flickered again.

"What on earth are you going on about?" my mother demanded.

"Let the fires fill the pot and the dirt stir the flames," my grandmother continued.

"Is that a spell?" I said.

"Not one I've ever heard of," said Pep, making a face.

"I was just trying to add to the ambiance," my grandmother shrugged.

Several of my family members looked ready to yell at her, but none of them got the chance. The next instant ghosts came bursting through the walls in every direction, looking frantic.

"The stupid Skeleton Trio is free again! They're terrorizing everything! Can't they just fall to pieces? Shouldn't they have become ghosts?" demanded Gus the ghost. His eyes bulged and his breathing came in sharp gasps.

The Skeleton Trio had been causing mischief since they'd arrived at the mansion, and no one had ever figured out quite how to rein them in.

"Where?" my mother demanded. "The Skeleton Trio is in the upper wings?"

"No, they're outside in the back trying to release the bats," said Gus.

My family members made noises of deep concern.

"Let's go!" Lizzie shot forward, she and Corey trying to squeeze through the door into the back pantry at the same time, both determined to be the one to save the day.

"What's the rush? The faster you go the more likely it is you'll actually have to do something," said Cookie, picking up her glass of wine and taking a good swig.

"Where did that come from?" Meg demanded, skidding to a halt.

"Don't be such a spoilsport!" said Cookie.

"We said you could only drink two nights a week. It's for your health," Meg chided her mother-in-law.

"You said that. I said it was six," said Cookie. "My inner ear translates nonsense into only what I want to hear."

"Where's the wine?" Meg demanded.

"She keeps some in the pantry off the kitchen," Lizzie called. Then she disappeared outside, on a quest for the Skeleton Trio.

"Traitor! Knew I didn't like that girl!" Cookie hissed angrily.

"I'm going to take the wine away," said Meg, getting up and marching toward the pantry.

Cookie raised her hand in protest and demanded, "How dare you!"

But Meg was already gone.

"That was a pretty epic performance," I said dryly.

"Do you think she believed it?" Cookie asked.

"Yes, I don't think she has any idea that the pantry is the smallest of the stashes you've got hidden around Haunted Bluff," I said.

"But it is two very good bottles of wine. She wouldn't have believed it otherwise. I had to sacrifice them," said Cookie sadly.

"Just behave yourself or we'll tell her about the library chest," Lark threatened.

"What kind of grand-daughter are you?" Cookie demanded, looking shocked.

"The kind I was raised to be by my grandmother," Lark shot back.

"Get them! The guests are going to see!" Lizzie ran back through the Magenta Room of Exquisite Furniture, also known as the dining room, saying she needed to get some rope.

Cookie sat back down.

"Oh yeah, the customers have no idea that we're odd, but this is going to tip the scales," Lark said, rolling her eyes. "By the time I get there they'll have calmed the Skeleton Trio down anyway."

Pep, who had to open the store soon, said the same, then asked Lark and me, "Will you come help?" The gift shop was open sometimes even when the haunted house wasn't. It kept Pep busy one way or another almost every day.

"This is ridiculous!" I cried, ignoring Pep. "What's been happening since I left that the Skeleton Trio is loose and everyone is freaking out?"

Lark and Pep exchanged looks.

"You don't think half the family rushing off to gather up the Skeleton Trio spells success?" Cookie said to me. Turning to my cousins, she added, "You might as well tell her. She's going to find out sooner or later, and the longer you wait the angrier she'll be."

"It only spells success if it's in a language I don't speak! Also, thanks, Grandma," I said.

"Don't thank me. I want to see you yell at people. They don't let me do it anymore," said Cookie.

"You do whatever you want and you know it! A chest full of wine in the library says as much," said Lark.

"Don't tell Meg about that," said Cookie with an evil grin.

We were just making our way outside when I had a sudden realization that made me spin around and head back into the mansion. What I had realized was: we were all being drawn out of the house. Even Cookie had hobbled out, muttering about checking on the chickens.

And somehow, amidst all the unexplained panic, it didn't seem like a good idea to leave the house unattended.

Lark and Pep turned around to watch me go, but they didn't say anything, or follow me back inside.

Picture this, you're walking into a haunted mansion and you know it's empty: Yes, it's spooky. *I* felt it, and I had lived there my whole life. More or less.

My heart was pounding as I made my way through the kitchen, which still smelled like the lasagna dinner we had helped prepare and eat.

As I left the kitchen, I found my hands shaking. Calm and relaxed I was not.

My footsteps echoed off of the dim walls and I could hear myself breathing. From outside came yells of, "Get a net!" and "I have a rope!"

I ignored those, knowing that my family would get the wily Skeleton Trio under control soon.

With a shaky breath, I pushed open the door into the hallway. It was mostly dark, with just a dim light filtering through the front door window. This was part of the haunted house, and it lived up to its reputation of being creepy. Shadows pressed in on either side as I moved toward the library door. The library itself wasn't part of the haunted house, but it was our first line of defense against curious guests who decided to roam.

I pushed open the mahogany door and slipped inside. The room was lit only by a fireplace and the moonlight streaming in from floor-to-ceiling windows interspersed with the bookshelves.

The books were old and dusty. Pep sometimes came in here to read, and I had a sneaking suspicion that Cookie often enjoyed a glass of wine and a good book by the fire, but she wasn't going to tell anyone that. You could tell *someone* came in here, because there were plates and teacups left from time to time.

Right now, though, it was empty.

Except that it wasn't.

"What do you think you're doing here?"

I screamed.

Chapter Seven

"Sorry, Jane! I didn't realize it was you!"

Mirrorz the vampire, looking concerned, stepped around a stack of books and into the open. He was the mansion's butler and had been since I was a child. He had gotten up there in years and did less around the house on a daily basis as the years went on, since there were lots of younger vampires to take on the workload for him. Since he was a vampire, it was hard to tell how old he was. But the lines around his eyes had deepened and grown longer, and the hollows of his cheeks were more pronounced.

At the moment, he held a duster in his hand. Mirrorz was always methodical and calm.

"Is this really the time of night to be dusting?" I said.

"It's good to get a little work done while your grandmother is occupied," said Mirrorz dryly.

He had me there.

"It's good to see you," I said. "I trust that everything is well?"

"Quite well." Mirrorz's gaunt face worked itself around into a reasonable facsimile of a smile. "How long are you back for?"

"I'm moving home."

There. I had said it out loud for the first time.

"Your family will be so pleased," said Mirrorz. "I know they've missed you."

"I thought something strange was going on in the house," I started to explain. I'd had a feeling deep in the pit of my stomach that I shouldn't leave the house unattended, but I couldn't put my finger on what had given me that idea. I hoped Mirrorz might give me a clue.

"There is always something strange going on in the house," said Mirrorz. "I've always thought that was part of its charm."

Just then I heard a commotion that signaled that my family was back inside. I waved goodbye to Mirrorz and went to confront them.

"Why are the ghosts nervous! What is the Skeleton Trio saying, and who let them out? Someone better tell me what's going on and someone better tell me now! And don't be sneaky about it, either!" I said as I met the whole crew in the hall.

"How dare you accuse me of being sneaky! What gave you such an idea!" said Cookie as she moved a bottle of wine further behind her back.

"Because I know you," I said.

"Nothing wrong with being yourself," Cookie replied. "Unless you behave like Lizzie," she whispered just to me.

"Let's go into the drawing room," said my mom.

"What if the ghosts hanging around hear us?" Cookie whispered.

The ghosts that lived at the Mansion mostly took care of themselves, but we still had to keep an eye on them. The whole family—except for my grandmother, who couldn't be trusted, and Audrey, whose domain was the kitchen—pitched in to help.

"Fine, you can wait until after, but we aren't putting this off until tomorrow," I said.

"Why not? We know you aren't going to forget," said Cookie.

"Because you're hoping that I will, or you'll buy a one-way ticket to Europe to avoid telling me," I said.

"Don't be silly! I wouldn't do that! Australia is next on my bucket list," said Cookie.

"They can have you, and good luck to them," I said.

"We'd best tell her," said Audrey. "If she's going to be here, she deserves to know."

For once I was hearing something good, and then I realized it wasn't good at all.

"Why don't you come with me to the gift shop and I'll explain everything," said Pep.

"Yes, that's a good idea. Let's leave the three of them alone," said Cookie. "I need a drink." She looked at her daughter-in-law, but Meg was looking firmly elsewhere and rolling her eyes.

"Fine," I said to Pep, "but don't try to distract me with selling T-shirts. I want an explanation and I want it now."

As it turned out, their strategy for keeping me in the dark almost worked; the gift shop was busy all night. We didn't have many chances for conversation, but it was enough for me to get the picture, and the picture was a grim one.

"So there's more unrest all around," I clarified, "but in particular, ghosts and skeletons have been going missing before we can get them here?"

This family kept secrets like some people keep marbles.

"The fact of the matter is, there's something out there attacking them. We've been trying to get them to the mansion faster, which is partly why Lizzie is training to be a haunt hunter. But so far it isn't working, or at least not well enough," Pep said.

I nearly choked on my shock. "She's training to be a what?"

"Don't act like you didn't hear her," said Lark.

"Oh. I heard her. I'm just wishing I hadn't," I said.

"We need more hunters, and Lizzie really wanted to do it. She's been working hard to learn the ropes," said Pep.

"How is Lizzie doing at it?" I asked, hoping to hear of abject failures.

"Fabulously, I'm sorry to say," said Pep. "Her statistics and percentages are top notch numbers for a witch."

Lark rolled her eyes. She'd flunked every witch test she'd ever taken.

"Of course they are," I groaned.

"She's brought in a lot of the most recent ghosts and skeletons. The group of ghosts that were attacking her in the hallway earlier were ones she had brought in," Pep explained.

Which explained why she was dressed in an all-black power outfit, I thought. She was either ghost gathering or clubbing. Tough to tell.

I sighed and shook my head. I didn't like the sound of it at all. "Why didn't somebody tell me? Why didn't somebody let me know while I was in New York that there were problems here?" I said.

"We knew you didn't want to come back, so why would we tell you? You'd either worry or tell us to stay out of it, and we really can't," said Lark. "We have to gather the ghosts and we have to get the skeletons here. There's no question about that. Now there's clearly something out there trying to get them, and it's a problem."

"And it's a problem for us, too," I added.

The two sisters exchanged looks. They knew I was right.

"Still, you should've told me," I said.

"Next time our very existence is threatened I'll let you know," said Pep.

"Don't be overly dramatic," said Lark, using her thumb and index finger to twirl the skull earring she was wearing.

"I'm never overly dramatic," said Pep. "The other thing you should know is that the supernaturals on the property have been more rambunctious, especially the Skeleton Trio. But the Trio has also been the victim of some minor attacks, and so far we haven't been able to figure out who's doing what."

Just then Pep caught sight of a young man of about college age trying to slip a mug into his pocket without paying for it. In a flash she grabbed her booking ledger, darted around the corner, swept up to him, and slammed the thick book into his shoulder.

"Ouch," he cried.

"Don't you steal my mug," she yelled.

"Sorry," he whimpered. He took the mug out, put it back onto the shelf, and quickly ran out of the store, looking over his shoulder the whole time to see if the curly-haired brunette terror was coming after him.

As calm as could be, Pep fluffed her hair a little and came back to us. "Sorry about that. Where were we?"

"Put the ledger down," said Lark, staring at her as if she had never seen anything like her before.

"I'm worried about the family," I whispered. "We can't really handle losing a lot of ghosts. Not to mention the poor ghosts."

"We'll figure it out. Your mom always knows what to do," said Lark soothingly.

Usually my mom did know what to do, and I knew it. But with ghosts going missing and even Lizzie being sent out as a hunter, I wasn't so sure my mom had things under control anymore.

After a night spent watching excited customers come in and out of the gift shop, I was exhausted. It had officially been the longest day of my life.

Not only that, my feet hurt.

I trudged all the way up to the attic, having decided against staying with Pep and Lark in their room. Pep's snoring was almost as bad as having a crazy ghost lady haunting me, and at least upstairs I'd have some time alone.

"Oh, no. What are you doing here?" Lady Oakley demanded when she caught sight of me. She was floating over by the window, her long dress and cascading hair tumbling downward. "Didn't you move somewhere else?"

"No, this is my new room," I said.

"Are you the one who can touch ghosts?" she asked, as if to make sure.

"Yes, so you keep me up awake at night and I'll throw you out," I said.

"I'll just come back in," she sniffed.

"Only once," I tried threatening. It was the only way to talk to Lady Oakley. She was unreasonable on a level with Grandmother Cookie, not that anybody could really be on a level with Cookie.

Lady Oakley snapped as if I had insulted her, and spun away. It didn't take her long to float out of the attic and leave me in peace. I flung myself on the bed and closed my eyes, but sleep didn't come for a long time.

Chapter Eight

I woke up the next morning with sunlight streaming onto my face, curtains being one of the items I hadn't remembered to get out of the left side of the attic. Grumbling at the early hour, I nevertheless tumbled out of bed in a hurry. It was Friday, which meant that tomorrow the haunted house would also be open. Lots could go wrong, and given that it was my family it was likely that at least half the things that could go wrong would.

I hadn't spent a lot of time in the attic when I was growing up, so getting from there to the kitchen in a mansion as large as ours was actually harder than it sounds. When I made the mistake of taking a wrong turn I found myself in a passageway I had never seen before.

Not wanting to turn back, I kept going, hoping to stumble on the right passageway one way or another. The hall I was in was hung with portraits of people I didn't recognize, but I assumed they were witches and part of my family history and told myself to find out more about them some other time.

When I got to the door at the end of the passage, it was locked. Out a small window near the door I could see the front yard, where Cookie was puttering around her cauldron despite the fact that there would be no customers for hours. I had no way to get her attention, and I wasn't sure I needed to. Yet.

The day was sunny but windswept; I could nearly taste the grinding salty air. The last glimpse of long summer days was fading.

At my back was another door, but that one looked odd somehow. For one thing, there was no handle and no keyhole. After pushing and shoving on it for several minutes I realized that I wasn't going to get through it.

In frustration I turned to walk away and accidentally tripped on the edge of the ornate rug that ran the length of the hallway; I hadn't noticed it at all until I stumbled it. I knocked my hand into the nearest sconce as I fell and landed on the floor with an "oof," just as a loud scraping noise emanated from everywhere and nowhere.

I scrambled to my feet in a hurry, only to see the panel of the wall that I'd been trying to open sliding away, revealing a secret passage.

The mansion was chock-full of secret passages, most of which I hadn't been able to find when I was younger. Then again, I really hadn't enjoyed looking for them as a child. But the architect of this place must have had quite a sense of humor. Uncle Taft knew about most of the mansion's secrets, but I had a feeling that even he wasn't aware of all of them.

Not willing to miss this opportunity, I went through into the darkness. The air was instantly colder, sending a chill down my spine. The door started scraping shut behind me, and before I could react, the white blur of the lighted hallway behind me disappeared. In that moment I realized—too late—that going into an inky black passage without any light or hope of getting back out wasn't the best idea.

The door slammed shut. Good idea or bad, I was stuck with it now.

"This wasn't one of your better ideas," said Rose the white cat, making me jump.

I could see blue eyes flickering at me out of the darkness, and that reminded me that I had a lighter in my pocket. I had brought it along in order to start a fire if I needed one, but I often carried one with me in any case. The mansion was always cold, plus you never knew when you might need to light a candle in a sconce, or illuminate your way down a dark and unknown hallway.

"What were some of my better ideas?" I asked.

"I need to spend some time thinking about that," sniffed Rose.

"I missed you yesterday," I said.

"I was on a mission," said Rose. "Don't get sentimental about it. You're the one who left."

"I'm glad you missed me too," I said. "How many dead mice are there?"

"You mean yesterday or in the last hour?" Rose asked.

"You're a bloodthirsty savage," I said.

"I'm a cat," she clarified.

"You know where we are right now?" I said.

"No, but I hope there's a new mouse here," said Rose. I could just picture her licking her chops in the darkness.

"I don't know how to get out of here, so we'd best go forward," I muttered.

"Great idea," said Rose, swishing her fluffy white tail. "You first."

With only the lighter as a guide, I started moving ahead gingerly. The passage was as narrow as most secret passages; they wouldn't be secret if they were bigger.

"How was New York City?" Rose asked.

"I missed home," I admitted.

"Don't tell me you're happy to be back," said Rose.

"I wouldn't be anywhere else," I said, thinking of what was happening with the skeletons and the ghosts.

"You shouldn't have tried so hard to make a go of it somewhere else anyway," said Rose. "You have everything you could ever want right here. All the mice in the world."

"Some people need more than mice," I said.

"You're right. You need a man, too," said Rose.

"What makes you think that?" I laughed.

"I know things," said Rose.

"Sure you do," I said.

"There are no cute guys around here. You didn't have a fellow in New York, did you?" she asked.

"No, I didn't," I said.

"You should really try dating," said Rose.

"Thanks for the advice," I said, rolling my eyes in the dark. I hadn't even been home twenty-four hours and I was lost in a secret passage while my cat gave me advice about romance.

"Any time," said Rose.

"How's Down Below?" I asked.

Rose was silent for a long time. Down Below wasn't something we talked about in the mansion, but I knew Rose went down there, and I always asked her about it. She didn't like the fact that I knew about her basement adventures, but I didn't like the fact that she knew that sometimes I re-wore my socks. Oh well.

"It's a little . . . different . . . these days," said Rose carefully.

"You mean because of the disappearances?"

"They told you?" Rose asked.

"Reluctantly," I admitted.

"I'm sure they didn't want to worry you," said Rose.

"If they didn't want to worry me, they shouldn't let Cookie tightrope walk on the roof," I said.

"We all have our faults," said Rose sagely.

"So why is the lower level different now?" I asked.

"They're just more careful," said Rose.

The reason we didn't talk about Down Below was that my mother viewed it as her own personal failure. The basement was a huge labyrinth. Skeletons and ghosts that she had brought into the mansion had gone down there when they tired of the haunted house, and now they ran an underworld—filled with gambling and dark markets—in our extensive basement. My mother hated it, but she knew it was better to have it here at the house where we could keep an eye on it than to let the supernaturals loose in a world that had no idea they existed, much less how to deal with them.

None of the family went down there anymore except every once in a great while when the furnace needed to be repaired. That hadn't happened in two years, so no one knew what was going on at this point.

Except Rose.

"How about the mice down there?" I asked.

"What mice?" Even in the dark I could tell Rose was grinning.

"There are mice in the house itself?" I demanded.

"No, definitely not. Forget I said anything," said Rose.

I shuddered.

I held the lighter near the wall and ran my hands over it, noticing for the first time that it was covered with a floral wallpaper unlike any I had seen in the rest of the mansion. The woodwork here was different too.

"You think we can get in there?" I asked.

"I don't know, I'm a cat," Rose muttered.

"Now you tell me," I muttered back.

I tried for several minutes to find any sort of secret doorway, with no luck. Unlike in the passage where I had fallen a little while ago, there were no sconces here, nor could I see any way out of the passage, much less into the space behind the walls. Tiring of trying to keep the lighter going while looking at the wall at the same time, I started moving again.

This had become a very long trip to breakfast.

I held my breath and tried not to panic. I was missing the first meal of the day.

"You want to be careful of the hallway. There are stairs," Rose warned.

"Thank you," I said.

It wasn't long before I came to a very steep and very narrow staircase. The thin walls pressed in, but I carefully headed down, because what other choice did I have?

By the time I reached the bottom of the stairs I was pretty tired of my venture. This passage hadn't led much of anywhere. I felt certain I had missed one or two secret doorways along the route, but since I hadn't been able to see them, I wasn't likely to get through them anyhow. All I could hope for now was to find a real door at the bottom of the stairs, so I could make my way to the kitchen and have my breakfast and coffee.

Lots of coffee.

"I think I smell bacon," said Rose.

I stopped to sniff. "I think you're right."

"Maybe I need to double-check it," said the cat hopefully

"I don't know what good that's going to do you," I said.

Audrey wasn't a fan of cats and did her best to keep Rose out of the kitchen, which meant Rose did her best to be in the kitchen as often as possible.

"And you wonder why I eat so many mice," Rose said bitterly.

"You expect us to feed you bacon every morning?" I said.

"Yes, if you're offering," said Rose.

"Let's ask Audrey what she thinks," I suggested. In relation to Audrey and Rose, brooms and shooing were involved.

"No need to be mean," Rose shot back.

"Here's a door," I said jubilantly.

Feeling a deep sense of relief at the sight of an ordinary-looking old wooden door in front of me, I tried the loose handle. It jangled, but nothing else happened. I couldn't see any light through the slit between the floor and the door, and it occurred to me to wonder exactly what was on the other side.

But I still didn't have much choice, so I pulled out my lighter and tried again.

"Open the door already," Rose ordered.

"Stop acting so much like a cat," I said.

"I think you're citing the myth that cats always want to be on the side of the door that they're not on," Rose said. "Forget the myth and open the door!"

"Yes, I'm totally confused about that particular myth," I whispered.

With no idea how to open the door, I simply started pounding on it. The bacon smell was very strong, and I thought that just maybe the kitchen and Audrey were on the other side.

"Who's there?" a voice called.

"Grandma Cookie, it's Jane," I called.

"Jane lives in New York. You're lying. I'm going to leave you there," said the voice.

I heard footsteps walking away and I growled. Ever so gently, I braced my forehead against the door and shook it.

"Cookie, it really is Jane. Please open the door," I yelled.

When I didn't hear anything in response, I started pounding again. It took several minutes before the door opened and my mother's frowning face appeared there.

"Cookie said it was a hummingbird in the wall."

"Not quite," I said.

"What were you doing in there?" my mom demanded.

"I found it accidentally," I explained.

"What are you doing here?" Cookie demanded.

"I was here yesterday," I said.

"I know you were, but I was trying to pretend you weren't. Please don't get in the way of that," she sniffed.

"How did you know about the secret door?" I asked.

I stepped past her into the kitchen and looked back toward where I'd come from. Indeed, on the other side of the secret passage it looked like a normal wall.

Just as my mom closed the door, Rose, who had entwined herself around my ankle, tried to dart back through into the secret passage.

"What did you do that for?" I demanded as Rose's nose narrowly missed being squished.

She looked up at me with guilt. "I just felt like I had to."

I rolled my eyes.

"What's for breakfast?" I said, turning back toward the kitchen.

"Don't act like you can't smell the bacon," my aunt Audrey laughed.

"I can't believe you're making bacon. I'm an old lady. I shouldn't be eating so much bacon," Cookie berated her.

"You shouldn't have eaten three pieces of chocolate lava cake last night either, but that didn't stop you," said Audrey with her hands on her hips. "The doctor says you're in perfect health and you're going to live for a long, long time."

"No thanks to any of you," Cookie sniped.

"Get that cat out of my kitchen!"

Audrey had just noticed Rose, and that had made her forget everything else in the world. Rose, for her part, was doing her best to sniff around in the lucky event that any bacon had been dropped on the floor. She even looked like she might be contemplating whether it was worth it to jump up onto the counter.

Whether she wanted to risk the frying pan my aunt Audrey was now clutching was anyone's guess, but in the end Rose decided against it and trotted slowly out of the room. She did her best to go fast enough so that she was just out of Audrey's reach while still taking her time to smell everything.

"That ridiculous cat," Audrey seethed. She replaced the frying pan on its wall hook and went back to the counter to continue forking bacon onto everyone's plates.

"The boys ate early and went outside to tend to the grounds," she said. "Lizzie went with them. I'm not sure what Lark and Pep are up to."

"I'm right here," said Pep, walking into the kitchen.

"Me too," said Lark, following behind.

The three of us spent the morning helping out around the grounds, where there was always something to be cleaned or moved or put away. Customers made a real mess in the haunted house, and everything had to be gone over and put back together after every open evening. The three of us worked until it was time for showers and lunch, at which point I went up to the attic to take a quick shower before heading back down to eat.

For a split second I thought I heard an alarm going off, but I couldn't place it and decided I must have imagined it. Shaking my head at all the noises the mansion served up on a daily basis, I got dressed and headed back downstairs, deciding rather rashly to take the secret passageway again.

This time I took the torch with me and left it in the doorway just in case. But it didn't take long to walk the passage and get down the stairs, and nothing out of the ordinary happened as I went.

Again I pounded on the wall and waited, hoping that Cookie wasn't in the kitchen trying to lie about what the noise was again.

When I emerged from the secret passageway, everybody in the kitchen was staring at me. It took a second for my eyes to adjust to the light, but when I did I saw that they were all dressed in black, and my mother was wearing a belt of knives.

"What happened?" I demanded.

"The Skeleton Trio got loose again," said Meg quietly.

"Do you really need your serious gear to go looking for them?" I asked.

"We already found them. They were smashed to bits," said my mom grimly.

Chapter Nine

Until that day, Haunted Bluff had always been a safe haven for the supernatural crowd. They'd come to work and laugh, and life at the haunted house had been good. With the Skeleton Trio obliterated we had entered a new and frightening era. It was imperative that we figure out what was going on as fast as we could.

On top of that, what had started off this whole problem was a slew of ghost disappearances. If we didn't figure out what was happening soon, the haunted house might have to close.

"Can't you just perform a spell to tell us what happened?" Meg asked worriedly. She was asking Cookie because Cookie was the best spell caster of all of us, even if she tried to pretend she wasn't.

"Maybe that would work for humans, but certainly not for skeletons," Cookie said. "There's nothing to attach my spell to."

"We have to deal with this and we have to deal with this now," my mom said firmly. "The other supernaturals are going to be desperately worried, and rightly so."

"We can't have it threatening business, either," said Meg.

We all turned to look at Cookie, who shrugged. "I didn't do it."

"We know that," said Pep.

Lark turned to me with a skeptical expression. "Do we know she didn't do it?"

"Oh, stop it. If I was going to commit a crime I'd be sure to do it properly and frame one of you so you'd stop bothering me," Cookie said.

"Frame Jane, she's the one who hasn't been here in a while," said Lark helpfully.

"Oh, thanks," I said.

"We can't just stand here chatting. We have to do something," said Cam.

"Look who's talking. You're only eighteen," said my mother.

"I've gone out on hunts before," Cam insisted.

"This is different," said mom, the worry clear in her voice.

"Yeah, this is definitely riskier," Corey confirmed. "Nothing like this has ever happened at the mansion before."

Kip had done the most hunting and was very competent, so when he spoke people listened. "This is different," he said now. "I don't know what's happening, but it's not something that's ever happened before and it's dangerous. The sooner we find out what it is, the sooner we can stop worrying about it."

"It really would be better to find out before tomorrow when there's a full moon," said Audrey. "If the ghosts are rained on and made solid, it could get really bad."

"What's the forecast?" Mom asked.

"Stormy," said Kip.

"I'm going with you on the search," I said.

"No way," chorused my mom and Meg.

"Yes, I am," I insisted. Being a haunt hunter was all I had ever wanted, and I couldn't understand why my mom wouldn't let me do it. If gender roles were actually changing . . .

"We have plenty of hunters, you're needed here," said Mom, her tone softening a little, but not enough to appease me.

"Oh, yeah, doing what?" I couldn't keep the note of bitterness out of my voice, especially since Lizzie got to go haunt hunting.

"We need a liaison between the stable ghosts and the house skeletons. I figure you'd be perfect. Ghosts seem to like you and skeletons don't like much of anyone."

She said that like it was a good thing.

In the end I spent the afternoon angrily trying to talk to the ghosts without yelling at them when they talked back. I was more successful sometimes than others.

"We don't like how all of this is going," the stable ghosts informed me.

"How is all of what going?" It took all I had not to roll my eyes.

"The attack on the skeletons," Gus explained, his voice shaking. He was floating above a bale of hay in the stables. "We're pretty sure ghosts are going to be next."

"My family's on the case," I explained.

"Now why don't you try saying something comforting," said another ghost.

The salsa dancing ghost nodded. Considering that she was one of the ones who had attacked Lizzie the day before, I couldn't get totally angry, because when all was said and done I might want her to do it again.

"What are your demands?" I asked.

"We want the early shift for this weekend night," Gus repeated.

In other words, the stable ghosts, including Gus, wanted the better shift at the haunted house on Saturday night. "House ghosts always get the good shifts," he added.

"They do live in the house," I explained. I'd been explaining this for the past hour, but they didn't care.

"And why is that?" Gus demanded.

"Because they don't attack the family," I said.

"I didn't hit you," Gus argued.

"Not for lack of trying," I said.

"We get one of the good shifts," Gus repeated stubbornly.

"Fine, you can have the good shift on Sunday," I said. I felt like this way they were getting one of the shifts and I still wasn't doing what they wanted, which was important to me. "Now I have to go inside and tell the house ghosts what's what," I added.

"Good luck with that," he said.

"Thanks so much," I shot back.

"It's okay to have you back, not," he said, sticking his tongue out at me.

I waved goodbye and trudged back to the house. I was still angry that my entire family had gone out searching for the skeleton pounders and left me here by myself doing grunt work. Pep was in the gift shop, but that was about it.

If they didn't come home in time for dinner, I'd be forced to eat whatever Cookie was making, because she'd be in charge of the kitchen. For once I hoped they'd be back soon.

Back indoors, I started looking for the house ghosts. It wasn't all that hard to find them, since they were playing cards in a Bluff haunted house room that overlooked the cliff as le-haunts practiced bad juggling nearby.

I told them that the stable ghosts weren't going to be walked over anymore and that they were going to have to deal with it. Then I headed off to check on my grandmother.

I wasn't concerned because something might have happened to her, but because with no one keeping an eye on her she could create a lot of destruction in a hurry.

As I passed the sealed door to the basement, a copy of the *Spooky Times* blew toward my feet. The *Times* was a sort of newspaper bulletin produced Down Below. Witches didn't have a newspaper, and usually the ghosts and skeletons went to great lengths to keep us from seeing theirs. Whether the grimy copy that had just appeared under the door had been shoved there or left by accident, I wasn't going to let the opportunity go to waste.

I bent down to pick up the paper before someone on the other side of the door could snatch it back into the abyss. Cold wind blew over my hand and I took in a quick breath, but I did manage to grab the paper before it could blow away.

After a quick scan of the front page, I almost wished I hadn't read it. On the top of the bulletin was printed in the largest possible type, "Danger! Skeletons beware! The end is near!"

"That's fatalistic, especially for a bunch that's already dead," I thought to myself.

Then I took a step and nearly tripped over something dangling around my feet.

"Rose! How many times do I have to tell you to walk on your own feet and not mine!"

"Apparently at least one more time," said Rose innocently as she faced away from me and stuck her tail in the air.

Before I could retort I heard a car drive up, tires crunching over the gravel out front. My heart started to beat more rapidly at the sound, which for some reason seemed ominous. It was too early for the house to be open for visitors. Everything here was swirling. The last thing we needed was company.

I stuffed the *Spooky Times* into my back pocket and rushed through the hall.

"I will not let you in," Cookie roared as only an old lady could. She was braced against the front door using her back, along with the deadbolt, to hold it closed as her tiny feet tap danced over the marble floor.

"Cookie, what on earth is going on?" I gasped, skidding to a halt.

Really, you would have thought I'd seen everything. The rest of my family was still out hunting whatever had smashed the skeletons to pieces, so I was alone with my grandmother, who was supposed to be cooking.

"Somebody knocked on the door," she complained. "I figured it would be best to keep them out, so that's what I'm doing."

"What if they want something important?" I demanded.

"They can't possibly," said Cookie.

"What makes you say that?" I asked.

"The young man didn't have flowers or chocolate. What else are they good for besides gifts of the floral or melting variety?" she demanded. From the other side of the door I heard a deep chuckle.

Shock spiked through me. There was a man on the other side of the door! I had obviously known there was someone, but I hadn't expected it to be a man who could chuckle like that. Was he young? Was he old? I suddenly wanted to know!

"Just because you're laughing doesn't mean I'll let you in," my grandmother yelled to the door.

"I would expect nothing less from the famous Cookie," said the man's voice. This made my grandmother pause. Any time someone suggested she was famous, she took notice. Her hand floated up and she carefully fixed her hair.

After a brief spell of indecision she reaffirmed her original choice.

"Maybe I'll just see what he wants," I said.

I inched closer to the door, but Cookie was wise to me and moved to block it.

"We don't care what he wants," she reaffirmed.

"You don't care, but I may care," I said. "Step aside or I'll ask Lady Oakley to haunt you."

"Lady Oakley doesn't scare me," said my grandmother, but her voice shook a little.

"That's because you never spent a night in the attic with her," I told her.

Grumbling, my grandmother stepped aside and let me unbolt the door.

Chapter Ten

When I opened the door, a gasp escaped my lips before I could stop it. Standing on the doorstep was a remarkably good-looking man. I had seen a lot of them in New York, but most of them were models who looked hungry, with overly-chiseled faces. This guy was different. He had black hair and bright blue eyes and I could already see just a hint of dimples when he smiled.

My grandmother peered out at him. "It's called the flower shop. You should have stopped there before you came here," she told him. He grinned at her, his eyes leaving me for the first time since I'd opened the door.

"If I had realized there were ladies at the house I definitely would've brought flowers," he said.

Cookie snorted.

"What can I help you with?" I asked. I was wary of this guy, not sure if he was here for the haunted house or the family, also not sure which would be worse.

"My name is Grant Hastings, and I'm with the Supernatural Protection Force," he said formally.

I was so stunned I couldn't speak, but my grandmother didn't have that problem. Sadly, she never had that problem.

On this occasion she squawked, "Why do you come around here! None of us are in trouble!"

Grant's eyes shifted to my grandmother and he raised his eyebrows. "I heard there was a problem with skeleton-smashing going on around here," he explained. "That's a pretty unusual occurrence. At least, to have it happen and not know the culprit. Usually they fight with each other in front of a lot of witnesses and something goes wrong, not this sort of murder by night. I was sent to help."

"Shouldn't they send a witch to help?" I asked.

"Not unless they think a witch did it, which they don't," he replied. His voice had taken on a steely quality that it hadn't had a moment before.

"My family isn't home at the moment, but you can come back when they are," I said, starting to shut the door in his face with Cookie's eager help.

He put his foot in the way and gently held it open. "I prefer to come in and wait, if you don't mind."

I had known he was going to do and say that, and I was terribly worried about my grandmother saying something horrible. He seemed to read some of that in my face because he said, "I have a grandmother too."

"Well then you should know how lucky you are," my grandmother informed him.

Reluctantly, I let the door open all the way. Grant stepped inside and took in the dim foyer.

"Nice place," he said.

I guess he hadn't noticed the extra coating of dust on the floor. The grandfather clock was especially dirty.

"We know," said Cookie. She stood primly, just as if there wasn't dust from the sixties in the corners and the chandelier wasn't missing several bulbs.

"Mind if I have a look around?" he asked.

I said yes just as Cookie placed her arm through his and said, "Let me give you the grand tour."

"Cookie," I said through gritted teeth.

"Dear girl, we have a lot of unmarried women around here, and how are we ever to get rid of you if we don't marry you off?" she demanded out of the side of her mouth.

"What does he have to do with that?" I demanded.

"He's male," she said.

"That's a pretty low standard for marriage," I told her.

"Beggars can't be choosers," she said. "Now go fix your hair. You look frightful."

Although my grandmother was pretending he couldn't hear us, our guest most definitely could. Grant was trying his best not to laugh and failing miserably.

My face went red and I decided it was best not to leave my grandmother alone with this man. To be fair, that was usually my assessment of her, but now it was imperative. We had an investigator here and that was really serious business. My mother would not be pleased.

"So how do you know about witches?" I asked him.

He glanced at me over his shoulder as my grandmother led him into the haunted house portion of the mansion. I had the distinct impression that there was something he wasn't telling me.

"I come from a family of witches," he said. "Men in my family are all haunt hunters, so it made a lot of sense for me to follow in their footsteps."

"Both my cousins are haunt hunters for this place," I informed him.

There were local haunt hunters who looked after the town they lived in, like my cousins and my brother Cam, and then there were regional investigators who worked for the network and government of the witches. Some were warlocks, but those were much rarer these days than witches.

Grant belonged to the regional force, which made him dangerous. Each region had one lead investigator, who was in charge of a team. I didn't know where this warlock fit into that structure, but I knew my mother wouldn't be happy that he had been sent to Haunted Bluff.

My mother had never liked the governing body, and she'd liked them less and less recently.

"This is a really great haunted house," he said. "It was used as a blueprint for all the other haunted houses in the area, right?"

We agreed that it was, and my mother was very proud of that fact. You could go to other haunted houses, but they would always be an imitation of the real thing.

We were now walking through a spooky bedroom that served as the introduction to the haunted house. There was a wardrobe in the corner with a ghost in it, and I longed for Grant to go open the door and be spooked. He must have known there were ghosts around, though, because he did no such thing.

"My family works hard at keeping the haunted house as authentic as possible," I explained.

"They've done a great job," he said, his head turning from side to side. He appeared to be fascinated. "I've always wanted to come here. My family has been talking about it for years, but I've never made it until now. When I heard you were having trouble, I jumped at the chance to come."

"Don't tell my daughter-in-law that, she's going to be mad enough that you're here as it is. She has fangs, a pitchfork, and a temper," Cookie warned him.

I thought it was uncharacteristically nice of Cookie to warn him of anything, but then I always thought it was uncharacteristic when Cookie was nice.

Grant glanced back at me, a slight frown furrowing his forehead. "Don't you want help with whatever attacked the skeletons?" He clearly didn't take Cookie's fangs statement seriously. Brave man.

"I think we have it in hand," I told him coolly.

"Is it that you don't think I can do the job or that you don't like the government?" he pressed.

"I'm sure you can do the job just fine," I lied.

"You don't think I can do the job," he said accusingly. "You think your whole family can solve every problem without anyone else. Typical."

Typical of what, he didn't say.

"We've done a pretty good job so far," I shot back.

"What other rooms do you have here?" he asked.

"There's a haunted library and the meat cleaver kitchen. We change them frequently so the customers and the supernaturals themselves are never bored. Aunt Meg is amazing with decorations, so she's able to make the house feel authentic."

"Amazing," Grant breathed.

I heard the front door slam and my mother yell for me. The three of us made our way back to the foyer, but my grandmother was intentionally slow, keeping Grant back and forcing me to go first.

When we got to the front hall we found my whole family, every one of them dressed in black. Only Pep was missing. I figured she must still be in the gift shop, oblivious to what was going on in the rest of the house.

"Any luck?" I asked.

My mother shook her head grimly. "There's not a trace of anything fishy. We still have no idea what happened."

Lizzie was staring at Grant with a look of excitement I had never seen on her face before, except maybe when she looked at Kip, who was her longstanding crush.

Meg was gazing at him too, and after a moment of puzzlement she glanced at me and asked, "Whose car is that out there?"

"His," I said flatly.

I hadn't paid any attention before, but now I took in the fact that he was wearing a uniform, all dark gray with a silver collar and silver cuffs.

The rest of my family wasn't so slow to notice such details, and my mother gasped when her eyes landed on him. "So it's like that now, is it?" she said. Her eyes narrowed.

"I'm just here to help," said Grant.

Cookie mimed a pitchfork.

"Supernatural Protection Force investigators are never just here to help," she said.

"If I had known a warlock was coming I would have worn a different outfit," said Meg in frustration. As it was, she was wearing pink pants and a blue and yellow shirt.

"Believe me, I just want what's best for the haunted house," he insisted.

"What's best for the haunted house is to let us solve our problems ourselves," said my mother.

"I think he could be a lot of help," said Corey. "We can go on more patrols now."

"Who's patrolling?" I demanded.

Corey shrugged. "Me, Cam, Kip, him."

"What about me?" Lizzie demanded.

"You're not ready for two and two patrols," Corey said dismissively.

It was getting late. I kept glancing out the windows.

Lizzie folded her arms over her chest and pouted. "I have a right to go out on patrols too. At least as much right as Cam."

"Oh, come off it. You just want to go out on patrols because he's hot," Lark said. Then she turned to Grant and said, "Don't get any ideas. I didn't say that because I like you. I said it because I'm not blind."

"Understood," Grant grinned.

"What's going on here?" Pep asked, coming in from the gift shop with a clipboard in her hand and her glasses on her face. She stopped short when she saw Grant. "Strangers?"

"He's an investigator here to help us look into the attack on the skeletons," my mother said, her annoyance dripping from every syllable.

"The more help we can get, right?" Pep asked, addressing my mother. "I take it you didn't find anything tonight?"

"You went out hunting tonight?" Grant asked sharply, suddenly all business.

"Of course we did. The Skeleton Trio incident just happened, and we wanted to get right on it," my mother huffed.

"And you didn't see anything?" Grant asked.

"No, we didn't see anything," my mother replied.

There was something about the way Grant was asking questions that was softening her. I was amazed.

"Were there any tracks?" he persisted.

"Not that we saw," said Corey.

"What about smells?" he asked.

"If there were any smells, the wind took them away before we got there," said Kip.

"I'd like a full debriefing, if you don't mind," Grant said. "We'll use the library."

Despite Grant's take-charge tone, everyone else turned to look at my mother for permission. I thought she'd have taken offense at his assumption of command, but she was already nodding.

So Mom and the four official investigators made their way to the library without so much as a by-your-leave to the rest of us.

Lizzie, still fuming, darted up the stairs without a word.

"She'll come down tomorrow. She just likes to make a scene," Meg commented.

"Maybe she'll stick to her room for a couple of days until she gets over it," Lark said, combing her fingers through her short black hair. "A girl can dream."

We heard Lizzie's door slam, and that made me grin just the tiniest bit.

"I don't mean to be rude or to interrupt, but the haunted house is due to open in half an hour," Mirrorz said, entering the foyer.

"Oh, no! We're out of time!" my mother cried.

The next few minutes were pandemonium as everyone tried to get to their places while simultaneously stuffing down cold sandwiches in place of a real dinner. I glanced at the closed library door several times, wondering what the four of them were talking about. I didn't like it one iota that I wasn't allowed to be part of conversation. I knew I'd make as good a hunter as any of them, but instead I was stuck being a ghost liaison.

As I tried to leave, my grandmother grabbed my arm, her knobby fingers and long nails digging into my skin. She was stronger than she looked.

"If you aren't careful, Lizzie's going to move in on your territory. Strike while the iron is hot! I tried to help you out by giving him a tour, but you're going to have to stop being such a sourpuss if you're going to get anywhere."

"And why again would I want to get anywhere?" I asked.

"Did you see his jawline? That's why you should want to get somewhere."

I sighed deeply. It had already been a very long day.

I stayed up late helping with the haunted house, because Corey, Kip, and Cam were preoccupied with the amazing Grant.

"Just think if we weren't here," said Lizzie dreamily as she helped move the old flatware that was used in the haunted dining room.

"Where else would we be?" Lark asked wearily.

Lizzie clearly wanted to talk. She'd been chattering all night, and Lark understood that her cousin talked even longer if no one else said anything.

"We could be official investigators, of course," said Lizzie. "We could travel the world like His Majesty of Magic!"

Pep snorted. "That's a myth for silly people like you who aren't practical," said Pep.

Lizzie glared at her. "He's real! He solved the Mystery of the Ghostly Haunting and the Mystery of the Silver Spoon! Everyone knows about him."

"The silver spoon was probably just lost in the dishwasher and some lowly paper pusher found it and decided to turn it into a story," said Lark.

"He's real! He's the most successful warlock in the world," said Lizzie.

"That's because there are only like five of them," said Pep.

"There are more than that," Lizzie argued. "Do you think Grant knows him?"

"Knows who?" I asked.

"His Majesty of Magic," Lizzie cried impatiently.

"Sure he does," I muttered. "He's totally real."

"I'm going to ask Grant if he knows him," said Lizzie breathlessly.

"You do that," said Lark.

Pep looked a little less certain. She followed the workings of the wider magical world more than the rest of us did. For the most part people didn't interact much, because that would draw attention to our existence, but there were instances where it wasn't avoidable. Anyhow, I was sure Pep knew more about other supernaturals than I did.

Regardless of Pep's uncertainty, Lizzie was clearly being ridiculous, as usual. Grant would probably laugh at us. It was people like him who did the real work, after all.

Wait, was I complimenting Grant?

Because they were so rare, warlocks were the rock stars of our world. The males in my family had a little bit of magic, but not enough to warrant warlock status. Witches with lots of magic were a lot more common, so the men were forced to find other ways to be useful, like haunt hunting and what amounted to police work.

The best warlock in the world was known as His Majesty of Magic. Far and wide, all the witching world knew of him. But to me his successes sounded too impressive to be real, so I considered him fictitious. If you were His Majesty of Magic, you weren't a haunt hunter. Instead you worked for the government as a special investigator.

It didn't take me long to become more annoyed than ever that my family hadn't told me about the problems facing the supernaturals even though I'd been in New York.

Now we had a government investigator landing on our doorstep.

Chapter Eleven

I was so excited to see whether Grant would still be there in the morning that I wasn't even worried about Lady Oakley when I finally went to bed. I was sure something would scare him away from Haunted Bluff, maybe Gus dive bombing him or Steve stepping out from the closet. There was no shame in lasting only twelve hours here. Actually, lasting that long was pretty good.

No, I told myself as I drifted off to sleep, Grant wouldn't last the night.

In the morning I flung off the covers and raced downstairs for breakfast.

To my complete and utter disbelief, there was Grant sitting amongst the rest of the family as if he'd been there forever. Lizzie, adorned with a sparkly top and an elaborately made-up face, had already arrived at breakfast and claimed her seat next to him.

Cookie whispered to me that Lizzie had been scouting out the breakfast table for twenty minutes waiting for Grant to show up so she could just happen to take her seat next to him.

Lark, who wasn't a morning person, was staring at the table angrily, while Pep chattered away about the latest sales at the gift shop. They were going great and she was thrilled about it.

Grant's eyes found mine when I came in, and they stayed there until I looked away. I made a point of sitting as far away from him as possible; just because my mother had warmed to his presence didn't mean I had to, at least not until they let me go out hunting.

I put bacon, eggs, and a blueberry muffin on my plate. Grant leaned over to look at what I had chosen. "You took the best blueberry muffin," he said.

Not knowing what the point was, I said, "How do you figure?" Was he accusing me of taking something I shouldn't, or what?

"It's the lightest and the fluffiest and it has the most blueberries risen to the top while not bursting and bleeding through the paper," he explained.

"Cool." I was baffled.

"Good choice." Grant returned to reading the paper.

"What are your plans for the day?" my mom asked Grant.

"I need to get going on the investigation. Smashed up skeletons are making everyone nervous. They're worried that this is going to spread beyond Shimmerfield," he said. "I'll begin by examining the crime scene again in daylight to see if I can find anything we missed in the darkness."

"We should talk to all the skeletons again too," said Corey thoughtfully.

"Mirrorz offered to help," said Cam.

"That would be really useful. He was the first supernatural here, so he knows everyone and can get information we can't," Corey said.

"What about the rest of you?" Meg asked

I searched my brain for something exciting I could say I was going to do and was coming up empty until I remembered that Uncle Taft had wanted help cleaning all the clocks on the property. There were hundreds.

When I told my mom that I was becoming a clock cleaner, she rolled her eyes. "He's so concerned with all the clocks," she said, shaking her head. "I don't know what he expects to accomplish."

"At least he doesn't give tours to haunt hunters and stir a cauldron like a crazy person," Lark said.

"Who would do such a thing?" said Cookie.

I was so unspeakably jealous that my little brother and my cousins were getting to help with the investigation that I decided to look into things myself. The only problem was that I'd have to wait until evening, when I could slip away and Grant would already have examined the scene himself. Hopefully there would still be something left to find.

"We gathered up the bone fragments," Kip told my mom. "Some of them were smashed into fine dust, but we're going to put all the material in the greenhouse."

Kip wasn't talking to me, but I made a mental note of what he'd said. The greenhouse had to go on my list of places to check.

Lark and Pep said they'd help with the clocks, and there was always the gift shop to be tended to, or grounds work if we ran out of clocks.

Eventually the breakfast crowd broke up, and my cousins and I went off to find Uncle Taft. This was easier said than done; we had to scour most of the mansion before we found him.

"Where do you think he is?" Lark complained as we scouted a couple of the upstairs rooms.

"Who knows, this place is too big," Pep said.

"We could try the roof," said Lark reluctantly.

Uncle Taft did like the roof. I shuddered.

The section of the roof that anyone could safely stand on was very small. Most of the roof tilted crazily and was old and dangerous.

It was the last place I wanted to look, because I hated heights. But it was the only option left.

And lo and behold, when we got there we found Uncle Taft.

The smell of early fall met my nostrils as we stepped out onto the roof. I could see leaves drifting gently across the yard, carried by the wind, and there was an aroma of salt in the air coming off the ocean.

Uncle Taft was standing by the edge of the roof with his hands clasped behind his back, giving the impression of a king surveying his realm.

"Hi, Uncle Taft," I said.

When he heard my voice he toppled sideways and did some sort of ninja move, as if he expected somebody to sneak up on him. "Who goes there?"

"It's just us," said Lark, holding up her hands.

When he saw the three of us he softened. "Oh, just you girls."

"Yep, just us. Nothing else to do but search for you," said Lark.

"Nothing wrong with that," he said.

"We came to help you with the clocks," I explained to him.

"What clocks?" he said.

"All the clocks you wanted to clean around the mansion," I replied.

"I said that so you three could get out of doing real work. I really don't want any help," he winked at us.

We looked down to see that he was in fact putting a clock together at that very moment.

"So we can go?" Lark asked in disbelief.

"Of course. You'll only draw attention, and I don't want that. I'm trying to hide," he explained gruffly. "If you stay you'll ruin my stakeout."

"Oh, okay. Hide from what?" Lark asked.

Uncle Taft looked up fearfully. "I can't tell you."

"When will you be able to tell us?" Pep asked.

"Probably not until it's too late," he said nonchalantly.

"Helpful," said Lark.

"He already got us out of work, let's not push our luck," said Pep.

Carefully we backed away and off the roof. I couldn't have been more relieved.

"What are we going to do now?" Pep asked. "We could always organize the gift shop files."

"You have GOT to be kidding me," said Lark.

"I have an idea," I said, biting my lower lip. "I don't think you'll like it, though."

"You want to go to the greenhouse?" Lark asked.

"Oh, no. We can't do that," Pep said. "We're not supposed to. It's part of the official investigation."

"Why not?" Lark asked; then she turned to me. "Now we have to go."

"No, we'll get in a lot of trouble," insisted Pep. "There's a government investigator here now. We have to take things seriously."

"You take everything seriously," Lark responded.

"I only want to take serious things seriously. This is a serious thing," Pep argued.

"We're going. Are you coming or not?" Lark asked.

"Of course I'm coming. Can't have you two getting in trouble without me," Pep shook her head.

"That's the spirit," I grinned.

"How are we going to find anything?" Lark asked.

"I'm not sure, but we have to try. We can't have skeletons being smashed up around here. The rest of them will get angry," I said, "and that won't be pretty."

"How are we going to get into the greenhouse?" I asked.

"I have a sneaking suspicion that the door would be a great idea," said Lark. "Unless you want to complicate this?"

"I do want to be very sneaky," said Pep with a grin.

Lark shook her head. "It took you a matter of five seconds to go off the rails."

"When we find out who smashed the skeletons, you'll be darned grateful," Pep insisted.

When we got near the greenhouse we slowed down and stood next to a huge, ancient maple tree, trying to look innocent and casual. The result was that we looked very guilty.

I took a deep breath. It was time to investigate.

"Where do you think the family and Grant are right now?" Lark whispered.

"They were heading for the scene of the crime, which is a lot farther out," said Pep. "They brought the remains in last night, so it shouldn't be too hard to find them. I don't think anyone's in there right now."

"Maybe we can pretend we're watering the plants," I said.

"We could try, but Cookie is always the one who does that," she said.

"Cookie is senile," said Lark.

"I wish," I said.

We walked up to the greenhouse, still trying to look as nonchalant as possible. Pep was sort of striding and tossing her hair, while Lark was humming a tune and I was trying to think of a good excuse for going into the greenhouse; saying we were there to water the plants wasn't actually going to work if anyone accosted us. I didn't come up with anything.

"I think we did that pretty well," said Lark once we were inside. The large space was empty except for lots of greenery and a gentle mist in the air.

"We handled it beautifully," said Pep. "I think we've found a new calling."

"Yes, we walked into a building on our own property. Good for us," I said.

"No need to be Debbie Downer," said Lark.

"Now, where are the skeleton remains?" Pep said.

"I think they're over there." I pointed toward the back of the space, where supplies were stored in a little room off the main part of the greenhouse.

We headed in that direction. Through a plastic flap door we came to a metal table on which were scattered the skeletons' remains.

There wasn't a lot left.

"Wow, these really were smashed to bits," said Lark, shocked.

"What sort of weapon could do this?" Pep said.

"I don't know, but look at this," I said. "There are no complete skulls. The only part of the skeletons that wasn't completely smashed was the feet."

"What does that mean?" Lark asked, her eyes wide.

"Maybe something was dropped on their heads," I said. "Everything was crushed except the feet."

"I never would've thought of that," Pep said.

"Or, they were lying on the ground and something landed on them, but didn't quite land on their feet," suggested Lark.

All three of us moved around the table, gazing at the debris. My heart was pounding with the knowledge that we could be caught at any moment.

Since the skeletons and ghosts were getting ready for the night's haunted house, the grounds were quiet. I hoped the silence would at least let me hear anyone approaching the greenhouse.

We were all just leaning over the table to get a closer look at the remains when there came a scraping noise outside the door.

We stopped and looked at each other.

"What was that?" Pep breathed.

"Someone's coming," Lark murmured.

"What do we do?" I whispered.

I looked around, but there was nowhere to go. The footsteps were coming closer and we had nowhere to hide.

Chapter Twelve

With only a breath to spare, I seized an old broom from an obscure corner of the greenhouse and tossed the dustpan to Lark so she could look busy too.

This was turning out to be a lot like every weekend I had spent growing up, ever. That is: me, pretending to clean.

I started sweeping the floor, while Pep got busy straightening the tools hanging against the wall. We got ourselves into character just as the door opened and in walked Grant.

He stopped short, his handsome face looking surprised, then very suspicious. "What are you three doing here?" he demanded. We had clearly interrupted whatever train of thought he was preoccupied with.

I kept sweeping.

"What does it look like?" Lark asked. She waggled the dustpan in front of the broom.

"I don't see any clocks in here," Grant pointed out. Damn the man for paying attention at breakfast, and the greenhouse for not having a clock. My mother really was failing this place.

"We thought we'd do some cleaning first," said Pep.

"And it just happened to be in the back room of the greenhouse where we said we put the skeleton remains?" Grant asked, bracing his hands on his hips.

"Hey, we can't tell where the wind will take us," I said. Even in my head I knew that was lame.

"It was supposed to take you to the clocks," he said dryly.

"We're just trying to help," said Pep.

"You should get out of here," he said, stepping aside to let the three of us file past him.

"We were just leaving," I said.

He held out his hand and I gave him the broom. "I'll finish up," he said, looking serious.

"Be sure you do. There was some dust in the left corner over there," I said.

Lark stepped forward with a sniff and handed him the dustpan.

"Maybe we should stick around and water the plants?" said Pep.

"You will do no such thing," said Grant. "Find somewhere else to 'clean.' This is potentially a crime scene." Without another word he turned and went into the back room.

It wasn't until the door had closed after him that Lark turned to me and whispered, "Did you see what he's carrying?"

"Yes, a hammer," I said grimly.

"Wait a minute," Grant said. He had come back out, but without the hammer.

"We didn't do it," said Pep, holding up her hands.

"Do what?"

"Nothing, I was just practicing," she said.

Grant shook his head as if he was confused, then started to say something else but interrupted himself with a surprised yelp.

We pushed forward to see what had scared him so much, but all we found was a white fur ball sitting on the floor and looking as innocent as innocent could be. I knew from long experience that it was the look that told you you were in trouble.

"It's just a cat," said Pep, grinning. "Her name is Rose."

"I just wasn't expecting a cat." Grant stared down at the small white animal as if he was terrified.

"She doesn't bite," I said. "At least not humans. At least not yet."

"Too many qualifiers for comfort, really," said Pep.

"How many qualifiers disqualify it from being comforting?" Lark asked.

"Any," Grant and I chorused at the same time. I looked at him and grinned, but he still looked fearful.

"You're a police investigator! Don't tell me you're afraid of a cat," said Pep.

"I'm not afraid of a cat," he argued.

"You look afraid," said Lark.

"Can he hear me talk?" Rose asked.

"I think only witches can hear you talk," I told her.

"The cat talks?" he asked.

"Of course she does," I said.

"Tell him I meant to scare him and next time I plan on terrifying him," said Rose. "Also, tell him I scratch."

"What's she saying?" Grant asked.

"She says hi," I said.

"Liar," Rose purred.

"You'll thank me later," I told her.

"That's not really what she said," Grant guessed, accurately as it happened.

"Don't worry about it," I said.

"I think I like him," said Rose.

"And his luck has just run out," said Lark.

"What was it you wanted to talk to us about?" Pep asked Grant.

Lark gave her a gentle kick in the foot. We didn't need to remind him.

Grant looked up and shook his head, "I honestly don't remember. In fact, I'm going back into the back room with the skeleton smithereens, where the world makes sense and cats are definitely not allowed."

He stepped around the cat and into the back room again, closing the door firmly behind him. It wasn't until he was gone that the three of us snickered.

"I think he likes us," said Lark.

"How can you not?" said Pep.

We made our way out of the greenhouse with Rose trotting along next to us.

"Thanks for saving us," I told her.

"Any time," she said.

"Now what?" Lark asked.

"Now, you really get to work."

We spun around to see Cookie with her hands on her hips.

Our amateur investigation would have to wait until later, but I felt like I was at least a step forward with it. I now knew that I needed to find out what was big enough to be dropped on three skeletons and heavy enough to crush them.

We spent the rest of the day helping out around the mansion to get everything ready for the haunted house that night.

At one point Lark stopped her work and pretended to think. "I can't decide if Grant is hotter when he's in command mode or 'I'm scared of a cute fur ball' mode. Maybe I'll ask Lizzie."

She laughed as I rolled my eyes, but her moment of lightness was surrounded by worry.

Everyone was nervous, not just because of what had happened to the skeletons, and the arrival of the police, but also because there was rain in the forecast for that evening.

It was likely that the rain would turn the ghosts solid and make them more dangerous, and no one was happy with that prospect except the ghosts.

We all dressed in costumes for the extravaganza. I refused to wear a witch costume. Instead I stuck a couple of fake samurai swords in my belt, tied a black bandanna around my forehead for good measure, and got ready to greet paying customers.

"What are you going as?" Lizzie asked.

We had run into each other on the wide, red-carpeted stairs. I heard her coming, but I didn't manage to avoid her. Next time I needed to be more careful, and faster.

"Just thought I'd dress up a bit," I said.

"That's what it looks like you're going as," she muttered.

She, of course, was dressed in full witch regalia. Admittedly the visitors loved it when she did that, but it made me feel vaguely ill.

"You really should try to do better with your costumes," she suggested.

"I'll think about it because you said so," I told her.

She continued on her way down the stairs without bothering to reply.

After a quick dinner in the kitchen, my mom gathered us all together. That included Grant, who was still wearing his uniform. I had a feeling he'd be invisible tonight, maybe off in the library doing research.

"Okay, everyone! Tonight's the big night," Mom announced, as if we didn't know it already.

She paused for effect, staring around at us with their hands on her hips, then went on. "We all know what to do. We've all been through this before. Just be careful of the ghosts and make sure everyone has a good time. The rain shouldn't be too bad until most of the guests have left, but we have to make sure nobody stays in the haunted house. There can't be any kids hiding out when we close.

"I expect this to be a late night for everyone, and I know we're all worried about what happened to the skeletons, but this is the first step in figuring it out," she said. "We have to behave normally. Tomorrow we'll resume patrols, and I have every confidence that we'll figure out exactly who is behind the smashing of the skeletons."

Lizzie raised her hand and Lark rolled her eyes. "Given how extra busy the gift shop is going to be tonight, shouldn't Pep have some help?"

Pep looked like she was about to blow her top at the suggestion. The only people who could help her were Lark or Cookie, but Lark didn't like helping and Cookie wasn't really helpful. My mother didn't want to acknowledge any of that, so her reply was simply, "Yes. Lark, would you mind helping in the gift shop tonight?"

Lark took a deep breath and looked like she was counting to ten before she agreed that she would.

Lizzie sat back in her chair looking smug. Usually Lizzie and Lark worked together on nights like this, but now Lizzie had the best job all to herself.

It was really annoying. Cam was the other guide, and he was very good at it. Everybody loved him because he was theatrical and funny. He usually dressed as a pirate to guide people, and tonight was no different. He wore a big red sash, a fake sword, a hat, and an eye patch. He was also practicing his pirate growl.

"Does anyone else have anything to say before we get started?" my mom asked, looking around and catching our eyes in turn.

She wasn't asking because she actually wanted anyone to speak, she was trying to close the meeting, but of course Cookie stood up to say something. My mother sat down slowly.

"As the oldest member of this family, I feel as though I should speak," said Cookie.

Everyone groaned.

"Actually, I'm the oldest member," said Uncle Taft.

"You don't count," Cookie shot back. Her weathered face looked like gravel raked into crags and rolls.

"Why not?" he asked.

"Because I said so," she scoffed.

"That's as good a reason as you ever have," he said.

"It's the only reason I ever need," she said.

"It was also the reason you gave for not wanting our children to marry each other," he shot back.

"Oh, don't get into that again," Meg sighed. "It's been decades."

I snuck a quick peek at Grant to see how he was taking this little show. To my surprise, he had a dreamy and bemused expression on his face. Apparently he was more amused by family banter than by cats.

"Anyway," snarled Cookie, "what I would like to say is, who took my wine out of the cabinet?" We all groaned again and stood up to leave without answering.

Grant was the slowest to walk away. As I was departing he turned to me and asked, "Who did take her wine?"

"I have no idea," I said. "It's likely that she drank it herself and forgot about it and is now blaming us for it. It's just wine providing her with an excuse to yell at us."

"We should get her more wine. A good bottle," he said. "Maybe then she'd let me in the house without your having to save me."

"I doubt it," I said, blushing. "Besides, Cookie doesn't need good wine to get drunk."

Grant looked offended by the very idea of cheap wine. I thought someone should tell him that from time to time it was delicious, but it wasn't going to be me.

I spent the night selling tickets to excited customers who lined up all the way down the driveway to get into the house. We always kept track of how many people came to the mansion for the haunted house, and I was pretty sure tonight was a record number for an early-season night.

I could just imagine what next weekend would be like.

The rain didn't start until late in the evening, but when it did it was more of a torrent than a sprinkle. We had given the ghosts strict orders to stay inside so they wouldn't be at risk of becoming solid and visible to non-witches, but late that night I glanced out the window and saw something white streaking past.

The supernaturals hung around outside the windows all the time, but something about the sight I'd seen felt off. I was very tired, and my eyes had long ago gone scratchy and bleary, but I decided I'd better investigate in case something dangerous was going on. A cloud hung over the evening; the Skeleton Trio had always been the life of the party.

Watching more carefully from my seat at the ticket window, I saw Gus making his way around the mansion. His body was stuck to the outside wall just under the roof, but little bits of him stuck out far enough so that they were being hit by water and solidifying.

Without hesitation I closed my ticket window and marched over to give Gus a piece of my mind.

"What do you think you're doing?" I demanded, bracing my hands on my hips.

"What does it look like I'm doing?" he demanded. "I'm walking a tightrope in the circus." He pretended to walk a tightrope, wobbling horribly. He was nearly as bad as one of the le-haunts.

"The circus would kick you out for lack of ability," I told him.

"No, they'd admire my sense of humor," he said, jutting out his chin stubbornly. "What is mere balance when you have laughter?"

"You're supposed to be staying inside while the customers are here," I said through gritted teeth.

"We kept hearing funny noises coming from Down Below," he complained.

I said, "You aren't in danger."

But Gus looked skeptical, and I didn't blame him. "We could be in danger. It's a scary haunted world out there," he said.

"You're a ghost and you work in a haunted house," I said. "You've seen scary things."

"Down Below is different. It's more like terrifying than scary," he insisted, his eyes going large.

"I'm sure it's fine," I told him. "They probably just don't like the storm either."

For a set of supernaturals who worked at a haunted house, they sure were a bunch of chickens.

"Are you going to do anything about the noises?" Gus asked plaintively.

I hadn't heard the thump, thump he was talking about, but that didn't mean anything. I'd been busy all evening.

"Why don't you just go back to the stable and stay there," I said. "You'll be safe out there, and I'll let you know if I find anything."

He brightened and told me that was a great idea. "I think I'll do that."

By the tag end of the evening the rain was coming down so hard it was difficult to see the cars in the parking lot.

The number of customers had slowed down as the weather had gotten worse and an all-out storm had broken free into the night. Finally I closed the ticket window and stood for a moment in the grand doorway into the mansion, watching the storm batter the windows as my feet and pant legs got soaked in the wind-driven rain.

I was exhausted, and after taking in the storm for a few moments I headed inside.

All around the mansion there were bumps and boos, the strange noises that the haunted house made in the night. With hundreds of supernatural creatures on the property, there was bound to be spookiness.

There was no sign of Grant, but I could see a light burning under the library door.

I told myself I'd been right about where he'd spend the evening.

"I suppose he got one of the nice guest rooms," I said to my mother as we headed for the kitchen.

"Of course he did," she said. "He's in the best guesthouse. I also managed to convince Cookie to leave him alone at night."

"I don't mean to alarm anybody, but there are a lot of ghosts outside right now," Lark said, smothering a yawn with her hand.

Pep and her sister had just emerged from closing up the gift shop, and while Pep looked fine and happy, Lark looked like she was about to throttle someone. Lark was much happier helping her mom with the decorations. She didn't like to be stuck in one place and she definitely didn't like customer service.

We made our way to the back of the mansion and met the rest of the family there. Mirrorz and Steve joined us as well.

The big windows gave a great view of the back of the mansion, and through the darkness we could see the ghosts out in the rain.

A crack of lightning sounded overhead and my mom's face tightened. "Well," she breathed.

"That can't be good," said Kip, gazing out at the rain and the frolicking ghosts.

"It most definitely isn't," said my grandmother. "But it happens from time to time. Nothing to worry about. You young folk are so dramatic."

"Of course we're dramatic. That's at least a hundred solid ghosts," said Lizzie.

The back field was filled with them, all hanging out in the rain, just floating around.

"Think they're going to attack us?" asked Meg.

"I doubt it," I said, smothering a yawn. "Why would they do that?"

"Right, nothing bad has happened to the ghosts yet, it's just the skeletons we have to worry about," Pep said.

"Exactly," I said. There was a lump in my throat.

"I don't like that they know about what happens when they stand in the rain," my mother said. Her voice shook a little.

"They probably knew before," I said. "I think it's fine . . ."

We waited a few more minutes watching the ghosts, but everybody was too tired to stand there doing nothing.

My eyelids drooped and I wobbled a little on my feet. As Lizzie and Cookie turned to leave I saw Gus through the window.

He turned around and gave me a little wave. I gave him a little wave back.

I did wonder about what would happen if it rained more often.

Something was wrong.

Something was very wrong.

I had come home just in time.

Chapter Thirteen

Despite how late I'd been up, I was up bright and early the next morning. The world looked fresh and shiny as it only can after a night of thick rain. The grass gleamed and the sun shone. Scarcely a breeze stirred the old trees, which had just started to lose their leaves. The world smelled like fall.

Everything appeared peaceful, and it should have been. But the actual fact was that there was an investigator at the mansion, and that meant that the peacefulness was an illusion.

I'd had a hard time sleeping, and I was remarkably hungry for first thing in the morning. Since my stomach wouldn't stop rumbling, I had finally gotten out of bed and gone in search of breakfast. Even if Audrey had yet to prepare her usual spread, I could still have a muffin and some cereal to tide me over.

Still in my PJs and not totally awake, I wandered into the cavernous old kitchen, ready to enjoy the peace and quiet. Outside, there was no hint of the storm from the night before.

I was halfway to the counter when I saw that somebody was already sitting there in the pale yellow early-morning sunbeams streaming into the kitchen.

I came to an abrupt halt in a strip of bright warmth.

My hackles went up. How dare anyone disturb my quiet coffee run?

Coffee was worth a lot. But talking? I wasn't ready for that.

"What are you doing here?" I demanded.

"Eating my breakfast," said Grant, glancing over his shoulder. He was dressed in his gray uniform and he looked like he'd been up for a while already.

I was acutely aware that I was in Winnie the Pooh pajamas. Hey, Winnie the Pooh was classic. I tried to order my eyelids to open all the way, but they needed the strength of caffeine to accomplish the feat, and someone was sitting between me and my goal.

"Good morning, by the way," he said. He was clearly far more of a morning person than I was.

Morning people can't be trusted.

"Good morning," I said. I grabbed a cinnamon muffin, poured myself some orange juice, found the biggest cup we owned, and filled it with coffee. Then I sat and ate and drank in silence until I felt like a human being again.

Grant appeared to be eating a broccoli and spinach omelet. I wondered where he'd hidden the greens so Audrey wouldn't see them. I saw him look with interest at my muffin choice, but excellent deducer that he was, at this stage of the morning he knew better than to comment.

"That was quite the show last night," he said.

"Yeah, the haunted house is really popular," I said.

"I meant the ghosts," he said.

"Oh, those. The rain makes them solid," I shrugged.

"I know, but I've never seen it in person before," he said.

"You haven't?" I asked.

"Clearly you've been spoiled here. I usually deal with skeletons. They're the troublemakers," he said. "You have an exceptionally large group of ghosts here at the mansion, you know that, right?"

I nodded. My family prided itself on keeping the best haunted house around, and the only way to do that was to have lots of ghosts. Until now it had never been a problem. They'd unionized, which had annoyed my mother, but Gus had pointed out that workers had rights too.

"You should go through the haunted house sometime when it's open and see what it's like inside," I said, taking another bite of muffin.

Before Grant could comment further, our quiet tête-à-tête was interrupted by the arrival of my brother in the doorway.

"You ready to go?" Cam asked.

He wasn't talking to me, but when he caught sight of me he said, "You look horrible. Haven't you showered yet?"

I mumbled at him to shut up.

"I'm ready," said Grant, pushing his chair back and standing up. Every time he stood up I was reminded how tall he was.

He took his dishes to the sink and washed them before he headed out. He was cute and he cleaned up. Need I say more?

Good thing Lark wasn't there to comment. Or even worse, Lizzie.

My mind was whirling. It had been so long since an attractive warlock had come into my life that I wasn't sure I knew how to handle it.

As he was walking out the door he said to me, "I moved the skeleton remains, by the way."

"Can't imagine why you think I'd care," I said, putting all my focus on my muffin.

Today was a big day for me. Sunday was Shimmerfield Market Day.

We would rarely have gone into town, except that Uncle Taft insisted that we not close ourselves off entirely just because we were witches and ran a real haunted house.

"They need to be reminded that we're here so they won't think we're weird," he explained whenever we challenged him on the point. "Or at least so they won't think our weirdness is that bad."

So every Sunday, some contingent of my family went to the local farmer's market. There were cheeses and breads, vegetables in season and cider during the fall. Usually there was a lady who knitted and a woman who made baskets. As Uncle Taft always said, it was a way to see and be seen and a way for us to stay a part of the "warm community atmosphere" to the extent that we could.

"Is Uncle Taft coming this week?" I asked as I met Lark and Pep in the foyer. Lark's hair was wet and she was just tying off her fishtail braid.

"I think it's just us today," said Pep, pushing up her glasses. "Uncle Taft doesn't come anymore. Last time he went he started telling a lady that the end was near and she got really upset about it. Poor lady didn't know not to believe him."

"Kind of like what he was saying to us on the roof?" I said.

"Yeah, he's getting nuttier all the time," muttered Lark.

"I'm not nutty! Look at the clocks!"

All three of us jumped as Uncle Taft came dashing into the foyer with his customary battered sword at his hip and an eyeglass hanging out of his eye. He was pointing at the grandfather clock next to the massive oak door.

"It looks the same as it always does," I commented.

"That's what you think," he intoned.

"Is there anything you'd like us to bring back from the market for you?" Pep asked.

"A date scone would be very much appreciated," he informed us.

"Sure thing," said Lark. "We'll see you later."

We didn't live close enough to town to walk to the market, and anyhow, we always bought a lot, so driving was the easiest way to get all the goodies back to the house.

Out in the driveway, Grant's fancy black vehicle was sitting next to our family's car.

"Think that could withstand a skeleton attack?" I asked.

"I think it would do as good a job as anything," said Lark.

We piled into the car and five minutes later found ourselves in downtown Shimmerfield. The market had already started.

"What are we looking for today?" I asked as we parked and headed down the sidewalk.

"Scones, for one thing," said Pep, leading the way to the bakery booth. We came away with plenty of bread and muffins to last us the week. On top of a collection of scones, we also selected a supply of cookies.

"We should really buy some vegetables," said Lark, looking around.

We spent the better part of an hour picking up everything we could imagine. Several of the townsfolk had been at the haunted house the night before.

"Nice opening weekend at the mansion. The SpookyBooSpectacular should be incredible! Your show gets better every year," said Mr. Gray, Shimmerfield's Chief of Police, stopping us as we struggled along with our bags full of supplies.

A zing of fear went through me whenever this happened, even though Chief Gray had always been friendly with our family and we hadn't done anything wrong. Housing ghosts wasn't illegal, after all. That would have required the wider world to acknowledge that they existed in the first place.

Still, somehow I always worried that I had a sign saying "The Garbos are witches" hanging from my neck for the police to read.

"Thanks for coming out to see it," said Pep.

"Wouldn't miss it," said Chief Gray. "Been going there since I was a kid. It's the best part of Halloween if I do say so myself."

"We try to make it as fun, I mean scary, as possible," Lark grinned.

"You all do an excellent job. That fat ghost is really something, and those skeletons always seem very real," he said. "I don't know how you do it. I guess makeup has gotten pretty good these days, not that I would know."

"Yeah, it's the makeup. We spend a lot of time getting the costumes ready," Pep lied.

"You all should be featured in a magazine or something," he said. "If anyone ever asks me what feature story I think should be done on Shimmerfield, I'm going to say your haunted house."

"That's very kind of you," I said, trying to sound like I meant it.

"By the way, did you get a new car?" he asked.

"A new car?" I repeated.

"Yeah, the fancy black number in the driveway. I notice cars because I'm the Chief of Police," he said.

"Oh, no, family friend is visiting," I murmured.

"I can see why friends would come visit you on the busiest weekend of the year. I bet they love the show. All that rain last night . . . Oh, sorry, the wife is calling."

Chief Gray's wife was standing by the apple cider and waving him over. After he left, Pep breathed a sigh of relief.

"You'd think after all these years the lying would get easier," she murmured.

"Funny, I don't find it that difficult," said Lark.

"Shocker," Pep confirmed.

Lark grinned, baring teeth.

We packed all our groceries into the car and headed out. I glanced back at the market once, wondering if anyone in town knew anything about the smashed skeletons. Someone had done it, and it was either someone already staying at Bluff Mansion or someone in town. If it was someone in the house, that was terrifying. If it was someone from town, I wondered how on earth we were ever going to catch them.

What we really needed was a suspect.

I got home and helped my cousins put the groceries away. After that it was time to figure out exactly what had crushed the skeletons, because I knew it hadn't been a hammer.

There was no sign of the police visitors anywhere.

Pep had to check some things in the gift shop, but she wanted to help hunt for whatever had obliterated the Skeleton Trio when she was finished.

We kept her company in the gift shop as she did inventory. It was a convenient spot, because we knew we'd be safe from prying eyes, meaning Cookie.

"First, where were they found?" I asked, hoping to brainstorm some clues.

"They were found outside. Where, by the way, they weren't supposed to be," said Lark. "Usually they just stay in the haunted house, but they were over by the carriage house, which is unusual for them."

"That place is so full of old stuff, we'll never find anything in there," said Pep.

"Still, we should check it out," I said.

One thing about living at Haunted Bluff was that there was always something new to be explored. The mansion was so large I still got lost from time to time, as in that secret passageway I had stumbled into before breakfast on my first full day back home.

As we left the gift shop and headed toward the back of the mansion, a closet door swung open, practically in our faces.

"What is the meaning of all these rumors! I demand to know!" It was Steve, confronting us in the dark hallway as usual.

"What rumors are those?" I asked him.

"All the rumors about skeletons being smashed and ghosts being next," he said. "As a ghost myself, I'm downright perplexed."

"Ghosts can't be smashed," I pointed out. "I don't think you have the same thing to worry about."

Steve was momentarily silent.

"You'll be fine," Pep said, trying to soothe him. "I'm sure the investigators will get to the bottom of it."

"We cannot rely on them," Steve warned us. "We must solve this as a family."

"We'll keep that in mind," I said dryly.

"Where are you going now?" he wanted to know.

"We're just taking a walk. Got to keep our circulation healthy," I explained.

"Ah, very good. Keep those legs moving," he said. "It's so sad when the circulation stops."

All of us looked uncomfortably down at his porous legs, then nodded goodbye and went on our way.

"I didn't want to say this in front of him, but does he realize that whoever smashed the skeletons is very likely on the property as we speak?" Pep whispered as we left the house and headed outside.

"I don't know," I murmured. "I just don't know."

The carriage house didn't house ghosts or skeletons, or for that matter bats, who mostly stayed in the cave in the cliff until we were ready for them during the haunted house nights.

The outside of the carriage house had once been white, but it had faded to a dull gray as weather and age had battered the exterior. Now the paint was peeling and the windows were covered in a thin layer of dirt, making it difficult to see inside and creating a very dim interior.

"This place is creepy," Pep said as she tried the carriage house door, which rattled in response to her efforts. "I think it's locked."

"It's probably just jammed," said Lark.

Pep dusted off her hands while Lark tried the door, and with a little extra shove it reluctantly swung open.

"It was stuck on the floor." Lark pointed to the concrete floor as we stepped inside.

It was a large space, dimly lit and very cold. I felt like I was entering another world.

"I haven't been in here in years," whispered Pep. "Look at that set of dining room chairs. You remember when Cookie insisted we get new ones?"

"I think she broke all the old ones just so mom had no choice," Lark murmured.

"Mom keeps everything," I said. "She always thinks we might have a use for something again someday."

"Which is great until we're trying to find something in particular," said Lark, looking around at the mess.

I nodded absently as we made our way further into the carriage house.

"Should we split up or stay together?" Lark asked.

"We should probably split up," said Pep. "We'll cover more territory that way."

With that agreed upon, we spread ourselves throughout the building.

The carriage house was larger than I remembered it, so large that I soon lost track of where my cousins had gotten to. I decided not to worry about it and tried to focus on the task at hand.

"There are so many boxes," Lark yelled, sounding downright concerned.

"I don't see anything heavy enough to crush skeletons," I yelled back.

It was true, unless one of the boxes had been used as the weapon. I doubted that was possible, because the box would have had to be filled with something as heavy as gold. Even with all the clutter in the carriage house, there was nothing remotely like that.

We needed a lot of furniture to make Shimmerfield Mansion functional, but some of it still ended up out here. I examined things quickly, but everything I saw had dust under it and around it, and there were no bone fragments. The bureau pushed against the far wall clearly hadn't been moved in years.

I kept going.

"Jane, where are you?" Lark called again. She sounded close, but I couldn't see her around all the stuff in the way.

I yelled back to orient her to the sound of my voice. A second later my cousin came around the corner and said, "There's nothing but boxes over there. I thought I might come search the furniture with you."

I nodded gratefully, and we started working systematically through the furniture, looking for any clues.

"I don't see anything," I said at last, squinting through the dimness. The windows were covered in grime, letting in only enough light to see by.

Lark shook her head. "No one has been in here in years."

It didn't take long for Pep to join us. She had also come up empty.

"Aren't you glad you came back here to search through piles of old boxes with us?" said Pep. "Way more fun than being in New York."

"The gladdest," I muttered.

"What about the piano?" Pep asked.

"The grand piano?" Lark asked.

"How many pianos do you see?" Pep asked.

"It's a possibility, but I don't see how it could have gotten in and out of here to be dropped on someone," I said.

Then a prickle of fear went down my spine.

I stepped around the piano and stopped short, giving a cry.

Looking back at me was a face.

Chapter Fourteen

I stumbled backwards in fright.

"It's just a dummy jack-in-the-box clown," said Pep, rushing to my side.

Lark brushed past me and walked up to the old clown costume that stood dusty and neglected on the gray concrete floor.

"It's like a circus asked to store its supplies here and never came back for them," I said.

"I think they used this when the haunted house first began, but we've gotten more scientific these days."

"It's terrifying." I glared at the clown, which looked an awful lot like a le-haunt from the early days. At first glance I had been sure it was real.

"Don't be afraid. Pep will protect you," Lark assured me. I rolled my eyes.

After that we searched through the furniture for a while longer, but we didn't find what we were looking for. If there was any evidence of a large object being used to smash the Skeleton Trio to smithereens, it wasn't here.

"What about upstairs?" I asked, pointing at the creaking boards overhead.

All three of us looked up.

Lark raised her eyebrows and said, "Upstairs is a completely different story. I'm not sure I've ever been up there."

"Looks like it's time for us to check it out," said Pep, brushing off her hands. "I can't believe the guys didn't think to look here for clues."

"Grant thought they'd found the weapon, so they didn't keep searching," I said.

"No," Pep said. "I heard them talking this morning and they had realized that the hammer wasn't the murder weapon. There was no evidence on the hammer. Grant said it had clearly been placed there by someone trying to throw them off. He sounded concerned about the sort of criminal this was."

"How did you hear all this?" Lark asked suspiciously.

Pep fluttered her long eyelashes. "I just happened to be hanging around on the second floor when they were in the foyer getting ready to leave."

"Remind me not to have private conversations unless I know exactly where you are," Lark said.

"Someone's trying to throw them off the case?" I asked.

Pep nodded soberly.

It wasn't a good sign that we had such a calculating killer on the loose.

The stairs leading up to the second floor were right in front of us, and we headed up them slowly. Even so, they creaked so loudly that any mice on the upper floor would probably scatter. I wasn't going to complain about that.

I did, however, tell myself to ask Rose to come out here and welcome the mice as only a cat could.

We had only been up on the second floor for five minutes when there was a rumpling in one of the corners.

Something skittered across the floor, and Pep screamed. A mouse went darting away.

"Where's that damn cat?" Pep cried.

After that, Pep wouldn't continue searching until I fetched Rose. Luckily, the cat always came to a loud, sharp whistle that only I could do, so I went downstairs and out the door and whistled away.

"This better be good," Rose said after she galloped across the field to meet me.

I couldn't help but grin when I saw her white streaking body racing toward me. She ran slightly sideways to make herself look bigger, which in this case served to make it look as if a snowball with legs was coming at me.

"Mouse on the second floor of the carriage barn?" I said.

"Count me in," said Rose.

She trotted along next to me as I led her back into the carriage house. "This is exciting. This place is usually blocked up too tightly for me to sneak in anywhere. There used to be a hole in the foundation that I could get through, but Cookie filled it up," Rose said bitterly. "Spiteful woman!"

"You can come in now. I'll even hold the door open," I said.

"And I can catch the mice?" Rose asked, her yellow eyes gleaming with hope.

"Of course you can," I said.

"Great," Rose said. "I welcome them with open fangs."

I may have thought that cats were sweethearts before I knew exactly what they were thinking. I would never make that mistake again.

We returned to the second floor of the carriage house and Rose went trotting away, sniffing around and looking for mice.

"There definitely aren't going to be any more mice showing up while she's here," I assured Pep.

My friend still didn't look thrilled, but she came all the way back onto the second floor after Rose arrived to protect her.

"What do we think happened? That someone smashed skeletons and hid the weapon up here?" Lark said.

"They could've hidden it up here intentionally, or just in the general area where they smashed the skeletons," I mused. "Like we said, it hit them on the head first and probably hit all three of them at the same time. That's a big object."

We spent another twenty minutes searching the second floor, with no success.

"Oh, my old doll collection!" Pep cried happily at one point.

"You didn't know it was here?" Lark asked.

"No, when Mom thought I was too old for dolls she just took them away," said Pep. "I'll show her."

"We share a room now. You are not filling it with dolls," Lark said.

"Oh, no. I'm going to fill the drawing room with dolls." Pep was grinning from ear to ear. "She should have gotten rid of them while she had the chance."

"Clearly," Lark said.

A creak on the stairs was our only warning.

"What is the meaning of this!" Cookie cried, waving her arms above her head as if she was swatting fleas. She was dressed in her witch's costume, complete with the broad-brimmed, pointy black hat. "Get out of the carriage house!"

"Why do you care if we're in the carriage house?" I demanded.

"It's obvious that she has a stash of wine in here and she's just worried we'll drink all of it before she can, which is probably by five o'clock this afternoon," said Lark.

"I have few pleasures left in life, and I'll thank you for not depriving me of the last ones," Cookie raged. "If I had a broom I'd tan your hide!"

"Don't be silly. You couldn't catch us or swing a broom either," Lark pointed out.

Cookie suddenly crooked her finger, and Lark went very still. She didn't move at all as Cookie marched up to her menacingly.

"Say you're sorry," said Cookie.

"I'm sorry," said Lark, her arms plastered to her sides.

"We were just looking around. We don't care about your wine," I informed her.

"So you say," she murmured.

As she stalked back down the stairs she waved at Lark, who could suddenly move again.

We rushed to the window and watched her walk back to the cauldron.

"She really told us," said Pep.

"Yup, put us right in our places," confirmed Lark.

"Be nice or I'll come back," Cookie yelled over her shoulder.

All three of us stopped talking.

"At least we looked around. I still think one option is the piano," said Pep quietly when she felt it was safe to talk again.

"There were no bone fragments, though, and how would someone drop a piano, not have it break into a million pieces, then hoist it back up here again, all clean?" Lark demanded.

"I don't see why we have to figure everything out right away," Pep huffed.

"We don't have to figure everything out," said Lark, "just one or two key details."

"Rose, what are you doing?" I asked.

I hadn't seen the cat since she arrived. Now I went looking for her amidst all the junk and odds and ends and found her crouched in a corner staring intently at one of the boards. Nothing else in the world mattered.

"Rose?" I asked. She didn't answer me. Crazy cat. "I'll just leave you to it and come back later," I said.

With that the three of us left the carriage house without having found what we were looking for. Still, we had eliminated at least one spot where the murder weapon could have been hidden.

Now it was time to look into all the other hidden places on the property. I was about to get a great education concerning my ancestral home, and I wasn't happy about it.

Chapter Fifteen

We had to hear all about the haunt hunters' adventures that night at dinner. Kip, Corey, my brother, Grant, and even Lizzie had spent the day investigating the smashing, and they were eager to report in.

Audrey had spent the better part of the afternoon making a delicious meal. There was pork stir fry, three kinds of pot pie, a big salad, and several other small dishes. I watched my brother fill his plate twice before I had even finished my first round. The good food was one thing I had definitely missed about home; wherever I was in the house and got hungry, all I had to do to find dinner was to follow the aroma of Audrey's cooking.

"I spent most of my day talking to the ghosts, trying to see if they'd seen anything," Lizzie said importantly.

"Did they have anything useful to say?" Cam asked.

"None of them saw anything, they just described the moment when they saw what had happened," said Lizzie.

"We really need a witness," said Kip.

"I'm not sure we're going to get one," said Grant. "Even if somebody saw something, they're probably not going to come forward. There's no benefit in doing so, especially if they know who the killer is."

"But if the killer knows someone saw him, isn't the witness going to be next?" I asked.

"You'd think they'd want our protection even more because of that," said Lark.

"The ghosts protect each other," said Meg.

"Not recently," said Grant. "I wouldn't be here if they had."

"What did you three do today, anyway?" Lizzie asked. She was looking at Lark, Pep, and me, but occasionally her eyes flicked to Grant, checking him out as if he was a piece of meat.

All three of us went still. I noticed a twinkle coming into Grant's eyes, so I quickly looked away. Then we all started lying at once.

"I cleaned the gift shop," said Pep.

"I cleaned out the stalls in the stables," said Lark.

"I started looking at costumes to see if any of them needed to be mended by Audrey," I said.

I saw Audrey's lips purse slightly. If I really had been doing that, it would have been because she'd asked me to, not because I'd just decided to do it on my own. But I knew she wouldn't give me away.

"Everything must be very clean," said Cookie before taking a big gulp of wine.

"Very useful," Lizzie said, and then went back to her meal.

Cookie took a great gulp of wine out of her goblet. My cousin's eyes flicked excitedly to Grant again and I saw her take a deep breath. Silently I told her not to ask him what she wanted to ask him.

I had hoped she'd changed her mind, but clearly she hadn't. Lark had noticed something was off too, but she hadn't quite figured out what Lizzie was about to do.

Pep, on the other hand, appeared to understand perfectly. She sat back in her chair, folded her arms over her chest, and smirked.

"Grant, I wonder if I might ask you an important question." Lizzie had gone beyond simpering to downright officiousness. Everyone took notice, including Grant. If he was still at the mansion by tomorrow, I'd have to give him credit for being more tolerant than anyone else I'd ever met.

"Of course," said Grant, laying down his fork and looking attentively at Lizzie.

Lizzie then glanced quickly at Kip to see how he was taking the attention Grant was paying her. But Kip was busy wolfing down an entire loaf of bread, and paying no attention at all.

Lizzie quickly looked back to Grant. None of this was lost on Lark, who just shook her head.

"It's actually something I've been wanting to know for a while. I'm sure everyone else wants to know as well. I know Jane, Pep, and Lark do, but I said I'd be the one to ask, because they're too shy."

As was a hallmark of Lizzie, she didn't notice how the currents in the room shifted with her words. Lark sat up straighter and opened her eyes, trying not to get too angry until she understood where Lizzie was going. But I knew that when she did, she'd be downright furious.

Mom and Meg, not to mention Audrey, were looking confused, because Lizzie was describing the four of us as having agreed upon something, which they knew couldn't possibly have happened.

My brother and my other cousins were too busy eating to notice the dire situation unfolding. Cookie had snuck a third glass of wine.

Goodness, get on with it! Even Grant's patience was starting to wither.

"I was wondering if you knew His Majesty of Magic?" Lizzie asked excitedly.

Cam, Kip, and Corey all exploded in excitement, darn them!

"He's amazing!" Cam cried.

"He's the best," Corey said. "A real warlock! He's his own man. He's only called in for the most difficult problems."

"Yes, we didn't want to ask, but do you?" This coming from Kip was the most shocking thing of all. He had used part of his daily three-sentence allotment on that stupid question.

"So, he's real?" Lark whispered.

Grant chuckled. "I know him. You could say we grew up together."

"He's as amazing as everyone says he is, isn't he?" Lizzie gushed, batting her eyelashes.

I'll be honest, I was a little curious myself. Lark was making a face now that she'd been clobbered over the head with Lizzie's agenda, while Pep was still looking uneasy.

"He's worked very hard," Grant acknowledged. "He's just trying to do his part."

"His part is huge," said Lizzie, in response to which the three of us snickered and even Grant's cheeks went a little red.

"I don't know about that," he argued, his eyes twinkling.

"Oh, no, it's definitely massive," Lizzie continued.

Lark choked on a piece of bread.

"He's done great things for the witchy community," even my mom agreed.

"He's caught vampires, he's fought le-haunts, if dragons were real he would have slain them," Corey confirmed.

"Someday I want to be just like him," Cam said.

Grant shook his head. "You should always want to be just like yourself."

"Is that what His Majesty would say?" Lizzie asked.

Grant laughed again. "That's the most ridiculous nickname, isn't it?"

"I think it's fitting," said Lizzie. "He's wonderful."

"So he is a real person?" Pep asked carefully.

Grant met her eyes and a split second passed before he said, "He is."

"Jane doesn't think one warlock can do all those incredible things," said Lizzie, tossing her blond hair over her shoulder.

Grant turned laughing eyes on me. "Oh, no? Well, it's might be true that some of the stories are exaggerated."

"Yeah, I thought so," I said. "No one can be that accomplished, especially at such a young age. It doesn't make sense. I mean, I'm sure there are some good warlocks out there, but what everyone says about him is clearly exaggerated."

"Clearly," Grant agreed.

"I'm sure some of the stories are false or overblown," I went on.

"You think the story of the howling hayfield is exaggerated?" Lizzie demanded.

Now I was afraid she was going to regale us with it, and as usual, I was right.

"His Majesty heard that a hayfield was haunted by a bunch of rogue ghosts," she gushed, "and they were terrorizing the local town and putting the magical people at risk of discovery. There was a big witch population there, and the ghosts had gotten mad at them for something trivial. So the ghosts were making a scene, and then His Majesty came to help and forced all the ghosts to leave! A whole field of ghosts!"

"Are you so impressed with that because the day Jane got here you couldn't deal with one ghost?" Lark asked her blond cousin.

"There were three," Lizzie sniffed, "so I don't know what you're talking about."

"Look," I put in, wanting to speak for myself, "I believe there were a couple of ghosts in a field and a warlock went to deal with them. I just don't believe there were hundreds of them, or that His Majesty of Magic or whatever he's supposed to be was the only one who could save the village. That's a bit overblown, don't you think?"

"There are really powerful witches who are famous too," said Lizzie. "This warlock is just especially talented."

"Men," said Cookie waspishly, putting up a conversational roadblock that everyone ignored.

Grant was visibly embarrassed, and I surprised myself by feeling a little bad for him. But I also thought that if he really knew His Majesty of Magic, he ought to just tell us something concrete. His Majesty, if there was such a person, was the most well known warlock of them all. He had supposedly saved the magical community from disaster countless times.

"If our situation gets worse, maybe they'll send him here. Not that you aren't helping," Lizzie added quickly with a glance in Grant's direction.

"No offense taken," Grant shrugged.

He returned his attention to his food, while I glanced at Pep to see what she might be thinking. She was looking thoughtful, but she elected to stay silent.

"Do you think this situation could get bad enough that His Majesty of Magic might really come here?" my mom asked tentatively. I could hear the hope in her voice, and it irritated me. We could handle this without some famous warlock showing up to save the day!

"Situations can always change. This one is already bad," Grant said, and that was the end of the conversation.

For the entire meal I had been waiting in fear of Cookie giving us away and mentioning our real afternoon activities. She never did, which was a relief. I thought she was probably saving it for blackmail later. But before we were through, she did bring up another contentious topic.

I was really so glad that my family behaved better when company was around.

Not.

"There's something of great importance we have to discuss," Cookie said, putting down her fork and knife after we had all eaten in silence for a while. I was already finished with my meal, but I had stuck around waiting for Lark and Pep because there was safety in numbers, especially when dealing with family.

Everyone turned to look at Cookie and waited for her to ask another question about one of her wine stashes. When she didn't follow up her announcement right away, Meg asked, "Is it to have you committed?"

"Don't make jokes," Cookie ordered her.

"I wasn't," said Meg.

"No, it's something else," said Cookie.

"Does it have to do with the Skeleton Trio?" Corey asked.

"Certainly not. It's much more important than that," my grandmother sniffed.

I wasn't sure what could be more important than murder, but I knew I was about to find out.

"Just tell us already," said my mom.

"Meg's birthday is coming up," said Cookie, grinning evilly.

Meg groaned loudly and sat back in her chair. "Definitely have her committed. I can't believe you're bringing that up. You know I hate my birthday."

"Yes, you hate your birthday and I hate having my wine taken away, but we can't have everything," said Cookie.

"Those are so not the same thing," said Meg. But underneath her irritation she didn't actually want to upset Cookie, so she added, "What are you thinking about my birthday?"

"I think something simple. Just a cake or four. Obviously invite the ghosts and skeletons and make it an affair," said Cookie. "We can't very well have a celebration and not invite them."

"We could just not have the celebration," Meg suggested weakly.

"Totally out of the question," said my grandmother. "Whoever heard of such a thing. Birthdays must be celebrated with large and colorful parties."

"Otherwise how would we know you love us?" Meg asked.

"Well that certainly wouldn't be the point of them," Cookie shrugged.

"So it's settled. We'll have a birthday cake for Meg," said my mom.

"Oh, very well," said Meg. "So long as it doesn't get in the way of Grant's investigation."

"Don't mind me," said Grant. "I can work under any conditions. I'm sure cake will only motivate us further."

"That's a lovely sentiment, young man," said Cookie. "My Jane has the exact same sentiment!"

She made a show of winking at me, and I felt my face turning bright red. On the bright side, Lizzie looked angry when she saw my grandmother's wink and my reaction. I tried not to smirk into my pork pot pie.

"I'd best start looking at cake recipes," said Audrey happily. "I was hoping we'd do something for the birthday."

"I like cake," said Uncle Taft, looking up from his plate for the first time.

"Did you find out anything else about the Skeleton Trio?" Mom asked Grant.

Grant's face darkened and he shook his head. "There's really no evidence to speak of. I've never seen anything like it. Whoever did this really knew what they were doing. They didn't leave any evidence at all."

"That's not remotely comforting," said Meg.

The rest of us agreed.

By the time I went up to my attic room that night, I had all but forgotten about Lady Oakley. When I stepped inside and turned on the light, her voice set me straight immediately.

The room was still musty, with cobwebs in the corner.

"What do you think you're doing?" she demanded hotly.

"Nothing much. Just coming into my room," I said, sighing inwardly.

Lady Oakley was standing by the window at the far end of the room, staring out at the dark grounds with her hands clasped gently in front of her.

I flicked the light back off so I could see her shifting form more easily in the darkness.

"Can't you do that somewhere else?" she demanded.

"No, this is my attic now," I said.

"Crying shame," she said. "Maybe I'll try to get rid of you yet."

"I wouldn't," I said. "You won't like whoever my mother sticks up here next any better."

"Will they leave the light off?" she asked.

"I doubt it," I muttered.

"Oh, very well," she grumbled. "By the way, you should really figure out what happened to those skeletons. The ghosts aren't happy," she sniffed. "In my day this never would've happened."

"Oh, no? Why is that?"

"We managed the property better."

"Don't let my mother hear you say that." My mom worked hard and did a great job. I never liked hearing anyone, ghost or living person, imply otherwise. "In your day you didn't have anywhere near as many ghosts and skeletons to contend with," I pointed out.

Lady Oakley didn't appreciate this observation. "Maybe not. Still, skeletons getting attacked never happened in my day."

"Did anything strange happen when you were running the mansion? Right when the haunted house opened?" I asked.

"Of course not," Lady Oakley started to say. Then she paused thoughtfully.

"Something did happen?" I said, getting excited despite how tired I was.

"No, I don't think so. It's certainly nothing." But her eyes widened as she said it.

"Now you have to tell me," I insisted, crossing my arms over my chest and waiting.

Lady Oakley drifted over to where I was sitting on my bed. "Something did happen a long time ago. When we first started here, obviously the basement was empty. It wasn't such a network of passages and tunnels that we couldn't go into it before it was taken over by ghosts and skeletons.

"The first ghost to go into the basement and disappear was when I was still here. One day he was working at the haunted house as usual, and the next day he had vanished. I was never sure why, but I thought it had something to do with one of the skeletons. Fudgy, the ghost who disappeared downstairs, was named Fudgy Bail."

I frowned. "You think a skeleton drove him out?"

"Something sure did, and it wouldn't surprise me if that something was still here. The skeletons have always been the most hostile. You live at a year-round haunted house and you didn't expect there to be spooky things?" Lady Oakley turned up her nose at my foolishness.

"Spooky and attacking the Skeleton Trio are two different things," I said defensively. The Skeleton Trio was no picnic, and before something happened to them I would have said that if anyone here was going to attack supernaturals, it would have been the Trio doing the terrorizing, not the other way around. As it happened, I would have been wrong.

"Are you going to be able to stop this thing before it attacks something else?" Lady Oakley whispered.

"I wish I knew," I said.

Chapter Sixteen

I had a decent night's sleep, but in the morning I had to face the fact that another issue with staying in the attic was the bathroom situation. The nearest bathroom was on a deserted back corridor on the fourth floor, just a few steps down. The biggest benefit I could see was that I wouldn't risk running into Lizzie. Still, until I moved up to the attic I hadn't set foot in that corridor, and no one had used the bathroom in years.

Once before I'd thought I heard the water running when I passed this deserted bathroom, and this time I thought I heard splashing. It was very odd, because as far as I knew nobody should be using it. On top of that, who would be taking a bath at this hour of the morning? Shaking my head at how strange it was, I nevertheless kept moving toward breakfast.

Lady Oakley had given me a lot to think about, and we had a busy week coming up what with preparations for both the grand haunted house opening and my aunt Meg's birthday. I had a feeling that before all was said and done, someone was going to have to venture Down Below. I would nominate Lizzie, because if she went and didn't return that would be just fine with me.

Lost in thought, I had only a split second's warning before a dark shadow rolled over my shoulder and I became aware that something was sneaking up behind me.

I fell to the hallway floor, rolled sideways, and ducked left, then right. Then I came up onto my hands and knees and bobbed and weaved until I could rise to my feet again, all the while trying to work my way around so that I could see my attacker. When I finally managed to twist in the other direction, I discovered that it was a ghost I had never seen before.

He was solid. He'd been taking a bath, and now he could hurt me. The one advantage I had was that whatever I touched became the opposite of what it had been. If I could just get my hands on the ghost, he'd go back to being immaterial.

A thick white hand started to reach for me, but when I swatted it away the ghost suddenly shifted and went vaporous. When I heard him gasp, I turned around to glare.

"Weren't expecting that, were you?" I taunted, feeling empowered because I hadn't died.

"You should get out of here while you still can," said the ghost menacingly.

"I could say the same to you," I said.

Without a word, the ghost darted around me and I was forced to move out of his way before he hit me.

I moved, then immediately spun around to confront him, trying to keep him in view and not let him get behind me again. But instead of continuing the attack, he suddenly looked defeated.

"You know this wing of the mansion is off limits, and the house doesn't open until nine," I fumed. The ghost's shoulders drooped and he plodded away.

As I tried to calm myself, I was startled all over again to realize that there were eyes watching me. I looked up to see whose they were and found Lizzie standing a bit down the hallway, eyeing me critically.

"I guess you've still got it, even though you disappeared to New York City," she said, trying to hide the fact that she was impressed.

I managed to stay standing until Ms. Priss disappeared around the corner. Then I collapsed against the wall, breathing hard. I had never been attacked by a ghost before, and that was certainly what had just happened.

In my own home.

I felt completely alone, and yet both Lizzie and the ghosts were all around the mansion, not to mention my family.

Having recovered myself a bit, I got up and tried to continue my progress toward breakfast. But now there was yet another pair of eyes watching me.

Tall, dark, and handsome was standing in the doorway, his broad shoulders slanted against the door frame. He wore a tight black T-shirt that showed off his cut, bulging muscles, and get this, not even joking, the T-shirt had a slash across the middle.

"Morning. Busy day?" I panted.

"Not as busy as yours, at least so far," he said.

"Don't you have anything better to do than lurk around the corridors?" I mostly said it to cover my embarrassment and because strong silent type wasn't likely to respond. Now that the adrenaline was wearing off, my knees were really starting to throb. I'd have to put ice on them soon.

"Not at the moment, no." He had a deep voice, because of course he did. "Is your knee alright?" he asked. "You look like you hurt it."

He started forward and I nearly stumbled back. How had he known?

"Yes, its fine." No. Ouch.

He smiled just a little. He knew I was lying.

"How did you know I injured my knee?" I asked.

"You aren't putting any weight on it."

Could if I wanted to.

"Can you?" he challenged.

"I should get going," I said.

He made a show of stepping out of the way so I could leave unchallenged, but what that was actually going to mean was that I'd have to hobble past him. Gathering my dignity from where the ghost had scattered it all over the polished floor, I pushed myself off from the wall and started down the hall in the direction that happened to be toward Grant. Grant tried to cover a smile, but he didn't do a very good job. I simply resolved not to look at him.

"I didn't know you could handle ghosts like that," he said, falling into step next to me.

"I thought you were staying there while I left," I said.

"What gave you that idea?" he asked. "I need to make sure you get where you're going safely. Cookie would never forgive me if I let something happen to you."

"You need to do no such thing," I informed him. "In fact, you should stay right here."

I felt certain he wasn't going to do as I directed him, but I never found out, because just then Cam yelled from downstairs, "Grant, there's news. Where are you?"

Grant suddenly turned all business and stopped walking. "Let me know if you need anything," he said. "You should ice that knee. We can continue the discussion of your ghost abilities later." With that he turned and headed downstairs to meet Cam.

I was resolved that we were going to do no such thing. But just like my knee, my resolve felt shaky.

A ghost had just made himself solid and attacked me.

My life was officially at risk.

I snuck into the kitchen and got some coffee and a roll, then headed back upstairs to my attic room. My cousins found me there later on, icing my throbbing knee and listening to a lecture from Lady Oakley about safety.

"In my day girls didn't fight with ghosts. In my day we let the men do the work," she fumed.

"But we're the witches," I argued. "Besides, I never thought I'd get attacked right here in my own home!"

"It doesn't matter! We're delicate flowers," said Lady Oakley. "We also don't *think*!"

"That's not how I look at it," I said.

"Then you're looking at it wrong," said Lady Oakley.

"That could very well be true," I said.

"What happened to you?" Lark asked, blessedly interrupting the argument.

She sat down on one of the big cushions set along the opposite wall, and Pep took the desk chair. I told them my suspicions about the ghost taking a bath, and how it had attacked me.

"I've never heard of that," said Lark. She looked concerned and asked, "What are we going to do?"

I shook my head. "The ghosts know they're not supposed to go searching out water. And yet this one did. He also told me I should leave the property immediately and never come back."

"Why would he think you'd do such a thing?" Lark asked.

"I don't know, but we're running out of time. I don't think the Skeleton Trio was an isolated incident, which means more skeletons are at risk if we don't figure out what's going on."

"And apparently so are you," said Pep quietly.

"Should we tell Grant?" Lark asked.

I close my eyes. I had hoped they wouldn't bring that up. "Should we?" Lark pressed.

"He already knows," Lady Oakley informed them, breaking my cover.

I opened my eyes to glare at the ghost, but she just smirked and said, "You can't expect to keep something that important from your cousins, can you?"

"It isn't important," I grumbled.

"Wait, he saw you fighting off a ghost?" Lark asked.

"He saw me, and so did Lizzie," I said. "Then he ran off with Cam because they had some lead in the Skeleton Trio case."

"They said we're not allowed to help with the investigation, but this is his job, and from what we hear he's darn good at it," said Pep. She was clearly trying to work her way around to doing what she wanted.

"Who, me? Bitter?" I said.

"Yeah, you. Bitter," said Pep.

"We can be helpful, though," I argued.

"Yeah, by staying out of the way," Lark suggested.

"The ladies' place is in the kitchen," said Lady Oakley.

I desperately wanted to avoid the family dinner that night, but I knew I didn't have a chance. My mother expected me to be there, and if I wasn't she'd come looking for me. Then my embarrassment would be far worse than if I just went in the first place.

Besides, I wanted to see Grant.

To combat the effect of people seeing me limping, I made sure to be the first one down to the kitchen. I was already sitting at the table by the time the rest of the family trickled in.

"How was your day?" Audrey asked.

"Oh, fine," I said.

I had wondered if I should tell my family about the ghost attacking me in the empty wing where he wasn't supposed to be, but I had decided against it. It would only worry them, and my mother already had enough to worry about.

"What's on the agenda for tomorrow?" Meg asked.

My mom rolled her eyes. "The supernatural unions want to meet again. They're concerned about their safety."

"What's gotten them so riled up? It was only the Skeleton Trio who were attacked," said Meg.

"I guess they think they could be next," my mom shrugged. "Be that as it may, we can't have them going on strike this weekend."

"This is the SpookyBooSpectacular extravaganza weekend," Lizzie explained to Grant, batting her eyelashes at him for good measure.

"Everything is going to be happening this weekend," he mused, ignoring Lizzie's flirting as if it hadn't happened.

"Looks like it," said my mom. "For better or worse."

At the rate we were going, it was definitely for worse.

Chapter Seventeen

Drastic times called for drastic measures. There was something Grant wasn't telling me, and that had to change. All my life I had always wanted to know what was going on. Even when I lived in New York City it had been difficult for me to separate from Shimmerfield. My excuse was that if we weren't all careful, Cookie would blow something up. And there was a good chance that whatever she blew up would be important.

After dinner I cornered Grant. He headed off to the library, and I waited until he was there to follow him. He and I had something to talk about.

"I think you should tell me what you've discovered in the Skeleton Trio case," I told him.

He was sitting by the fire with papers spread out on a table in front of him. He had moved the table from underneath one of the windows to a spot closer to the bookshelf that housed materials about black magic and beasts. He didn't bother covering any of the papers when I came in.

He looked up at me in surprise. Had he really not thought I'd ask? The lamp cast a shadow on his face, making his features appear even more chiseled than they usually did. "I can see your leg is doing better."

"My leg is fine," I snapped. "What isn't fine is your being here investigating and not sharing the information with us."

"I'm actually sharing it with a lot of people, just not you," he said.

"Why not me?" I persisted, trying not to be too rude. Yet.

"You have no reason to know," he said calmly.

"Sure I do! This is my home," I said. "Something is attacking my home, and I have a right to know what you're finding out about it."

"Are you telling me you really don't know what it is?" he asked.

"Of course I don't know what it is," I replied. Then I asked grudgingly, "You do?"

"Why do you sound so surprised?" he said. "Don't you think I'm good at my job?"

I gave him the famous Garbo Glare and waited him out. No way was I going to tell him I had heard of him before, and that what I had heard was that he was super impressive, he was amazing, he was the most talented warlock in a generation. There had been so much praise aimed in his direction that I felt certain it couldn't all be true.

He must have seen some of these thoughts pass across my face, because he smiled.

"We think it's a band of skeletons, or maybe vampires, or maybe both, known as the Root of All Evil," he said.

I laughed out loud. My whole body shook with amusement, and it took me several seconds to calm down.

"You've got to be joking," I said.

He didn't look like he was.

"How is that the kind of name you give a gang?" I wondered.

He shrugged. "That's what they call themselves. They're supernaturals who don't like the way the haunted house is run, so they're determined to do it differently. The only problem is that when they're opposed, they smash things to nothing."

"So, do the ghosts have a reason to be afraid?"

Grant stared hard at me for several seconds, the darkness surrounding his face shifting as the fire rose and fell. His heavy gaze made me squirm uncomfortably, but I couldn't look away.

"Probably," he said after a while. "Given what happened to the Skeleton Trio, I'd say yes."

"What will you do as your next step?" I asked.

"I can't tell you that," he said, sitting up a little. His relaxed posture was gone, and I could see that he was closing himself off to me.

I looked at him and realized that he actually meant it. He wasn't going to tell me anything more.

"Look, I can't tell you anything else," Grant repeated when I didn't respond the first time.

"I don't want to know anything else," I informed him haughtily. *I'll just find it out for myself*, I thought silently. Then I turned around and stormed away, not caring how silly I was being. I was going to conduct my own investigation whether Grant liked it or not. Now I just had to figure out how one conducted an investigation . . .

I turned and looked at Grant one more time on my way out the door. I had the distinct impression that I didn't know anything about the man at all.

The next morning I decided I needed to interview the ghosts, vampires, le-haunts, and skeletons myself. The Skeleton Trio had been extra rambunctious, but all the skeletons were friends with each other, so I hoped someone would have some useful information. I could start with Mirrorz. He wasn't a skeleton, but he had been at the mansion the longest and was the easiest to talk to.

There was one possibility I didn't want to consider. What if the murderer was Grant? He'd just showed up out of the blue, claiming he was there to help. I thought that the possibility of his being the culprit was unlikely, but I couldn't dismiss it entirely. The timing was too perfect for that.

Maybe he was trusting other family members with information about the investigation, but until I knew everything, he'd remain a suspect in my mind.

Meanwhile, my mom and Aunt Meg were meeting with the supernatural union members. Judging from the thumps on the wall and the shouting, it wasn't going well. With the extravaganza only days away, a boycott was the last thing my mom needed, and the unions knew it. The demands were likely to be outrageous.

After searching for a while, I found the ancient vampire in the Silver Room, where we kept all sorts of fancy silver cutlery, dishes, and household goods. Sunlight streaming through the large windows refracted and made a million sparkling crystals on the floor.

"Hello, Jane," Mirrorz said, greeting me warmly without even turning around to see who had come in.

"How did you do that?" I asked, and he held up the silver platter he was polishing by way of answer.

I sat down across from him. He grinned at me and I grinned back. "Polishing the silver again?" I asked.

"Your grandmother doesn't seem to like to leave it alone," he sighed.

"That's so surprising," I said dryly.

"Isn't it?" he said. When he bent his head and continued polishing, I picked up a spare rag and started to help.

"What is it I can help you with?" he asked.

"I was hoping you could tell me more about the Skeleton Trio."

I was relieved when he didn't act the least bit surprised. Mirrorz was very hard to surprise.

"What is it you want to know?" he asked.

"Everything," I told him.

"Why?"

"I thought I'd conduct my own investigation," I said.

"You don't trust the official force?" he asked.

I faltered. As a matter of fact I didn't, but separate from that, I wanted to know for myself what was going on, and no one was telling me anything useful.

"I just think an investigation might go more smoothly if it were conducted by somebody who had grown up here at the haunted house," I said.

"Can't argue with that," Mirrorz said.

"So about the Skeleton Trio?" I said. "Do you have any idea why they would be targeted specifically?"

This was something that had been nagging at me, and I hadn't been able to put my finger on why.

"I suppose there are two options," he said. "Either they did something wrong, or they were just in the wrong place at the wrong time."

"When you say they were in the wrong place at the wrong time, you mean they saw something they shouldn't have?"

"Maybe something like that," he shrugged.

"But what would they have seen?" I wondered.

"That I can't tell you," he said. "Although it could have something to do with Down Below."

This was the second time Down Below had been mentioned to me in twenty-four hours. If it happened a third time I'd actually have to go down there and find out what was what these days in the mansion's underbelly. And nobody wanted that, least of all me.

"What would they have been doing out there at that time of night, though?" I said.

"They probably would've been digging up their treasure," he said.

"What treasure?" I asked.

Mirrorz snorted. "Those three slowly stole stuff from all around the house, buried it in the back yard, and waited for one of your family to notice. None of you ever have except for Cookie, and nobody believes her."

I gaped at him. "You mean Cookie realized they were stealing and told my mom, and my mom hasn't done anything?"

"They only ever stole small items, so it was hard for your family to notice. Cookie seems to have a catalog of every item on this property, and don't ever let her tell you differently."

"I can believe she does," I said dryly.

Mirrorz chuckled and asked me how I knew.

"Because she likes to keep score, and one of the ways she does it is by keeping track of everyone's stuff," I said.

Mirrorz nodded as if that made perfect sense to him. "Maybe you should ask her what they were stealing," he suggested.

"Maybe I will," I said. But the thought was terrifying. "You think they were out there hiding their stolen goods and they ran into something they weren't supposed to see?"

"I cannot say for sure, but I'd be surprised if whoever killed them didn't know they were going to be there," he said.

"How could my family and the official police miss the buried stuff?"

"I have no idea," he said. "That's really all I know."

I chatted with Mirrorz for a little longer, then excused myself. I had to talk to Cookie, and I had to go look at this crime scene for myself, even if Grant didn't like it.

Cookie wasn't at the cauldron out front, but on my way there I ran into Lark and Pep carrying boxes of new products to the gift shop. Lark was grumbling about having to help with the shop given how much she hated it, but she was still working.

When I told them about my mission, they both dropped their boxes to come help me.

Having searched everywhere for Cookie with no luck, we decided to go out to the crime scene. It was marked with a big white line in the grass, and someone had put a stake in the ground with a sign that said, "Off limits."

"Oh, well," said Pep.

Without a moment's hesitation she went around the sign. As she stepped over the white line she shivered a little, as if it had shocked her.

"Magic?" I asked.

She nodded. "Probably your mom's."

"We don't have a lot of time," said Lark, glancing over her shoulder.

The three of us made our way quickly to the spot where the skeletons had been smashed and started to look around. As far as I could see, it all just looked like dirt.

"What about those shrubs over there?" Lark asked.

"The ones Meg planted a couple of years ago?" I asked.

The shrubs stood awkwardly by themselves, with three fake gravestones in front of them. My aunt had put them out there in case anybody looked through the back windows of the haunted house and saw something they shouldn't. She wanted the ambiance.

We searched around the scraggly green shrubs as the shadows started to lengthen and the sky went from blue to dull pink.

"I think this is all just dirt," Lark said.

"Mirrorz said the Skeleton Trio had a stash of stolen items somewhere on the grounds," I mused.

"Reason enough to kill?" Pep wondered.

"He speculated that their stash was around here somewhere, because that might have been what they were outside for."

We were still looking around when I saw my mother stomping out of the back of the house toward us, flanked by Corey and Kip.

"I guess they aren't out of town," Lark muttered.

"Just what do you think you're doing out here?" my mother demanded. She was marching across the grass toward us, her facing matching a stormy night. "Does everything have to be difficult? This areas is off limits."

"Sorry, we didn't know that," said Pep.

"You can read," said Corey, pointing to the prominent sign.

"Yeah, but sometimes I choose not to, like, if I close my eyes and walk past," said Lark.

"Get away from that crime scene right now," my mom ordered.

The three of us slowly stepped back over the white line.

"Really, you're just making this harder," said Kip quietly

"I'm sure you can manage," I said.

Kip and Corey didn't stick around to keep lecturing us; they had gotten into enough trouble themselves over the years to know that Mom was going to yell at us, so they didn't have to bother. The fact that they had done plenty worse in their day was irrelevant.

"We have an investigator here. Don't get in his way. The harder it is for him to do his job, the longer he might be around, and no one wants that," Mom huffed.

Without waiting for a response, she spun around and headed back to the house.

After that, Mom stayed in the kitchen with Meg and Audrey for a long time. Audrey was making different kinds of cake for the party and having Meg try them. Meg thought all the options were delicious, making it very difficult for Audrey to choose.

"Really, isn't there enough going on around here without you three causing more difficulties?" my mom asked when we finally walked back into the house.

"What did they do now?" asked Meg.

Mom told them, but instead of looking annoyed, Meg just looked amused.

"So? We did a lot worse when we were younger," she said.

"We most certainly did not," Mom insisted. "If we'd been told not to interfere with an investigation, then we wouldn't have. Really, you talk as if we habitually disobeyed our elders."

"Well, you did." Cookie's voice came floating from above, and we all looked up to see her sitting on one of the beams. The kitchen had a very high ceiling, above which was a loft where we stored large quantities of packaged goods. We could see Cookie's knobby knees and pulled-up socks as she swung her legs in the air.

"Cookie, get down from there before you fall down," Audrey cried.

"You'd like that, wouldn't you? If I just tumbled down and you didn't have to put up with your batty old mother-in-law anymore."

"No, Cookie, I wouldn't like that at all," was Audrey's retort.

"What are you doing up there, anyhow?" Meg said.

"This is where Audrey hid the jam, and I want some," said Cookie, waving a large jar of jam in the air and looking triumphant.

"Great, now will you get down?" my mom demanded.

"Oh, very well." My grandmother scooted along the beam until she got to the rafter, then shimmied down to where the ladder was. Once her feet were firmly on it I went and held the base steady so she could climb down safely.

"Thanks," she said once she was back at our level. "Were you looking for me earlier?"

"How did you know?" I asked.

"I saw you walk out to the cauldron," she said.

"And you didn't call out to me? Why not?" I demanded.

"Seemed easier not to," Cookie shrugged.

I rolled my eyes. Typical.

"How were we difficult when we were younger?" my mom demanded, not willing to let it go.

"You were trouble. Why do you think I didn't want my son to marry you?" Cookie said.

My mother was used to hearing this line of thinking, and she just shook her head. "I was far less trouble than that son of yours. If there was any mischief to get up to at all, he was right there in front leading the way," she said.

"My son never got up to any trouble! He was a good boy," Cookie argued.

"Ha! You're lying! Are you forgetting the time he stuck the cat in the tree on purpose?" Audrey asked. "Bill told me all about it."

"I didn't know anything like that happened," said Cookie.

"Bill said you were the one who climbed the tree to get it down," said Audrey.

"I certainly don't remember that," sniffed Cookie.

"Of course not," said Audrey. "And what about the time Bill hid in the attic and triggered a property-wide search? You thought something had happened to him, right? Like maybe a group of skeletons had taken him Down Below?"

My grandmother's face paled. That sounded awfully similar to what Grant had been saying the night before. There was a troublesome gang of skeletons and they were causing . . . trouble.

"AHH!" Suddenly Audrey let out a loud scream.

"What!" all of us chorused, as everyone but Cookie ran to try to help her.

Rose, ignoring the ruckus, trotted calmly over to me, purring loudly enough for all of us to hear.

"Get that cat OUT of my kitchen! Now!" Audrey yelled.

I quickly scooped Rose up and made for the door. This conversation was over, and Rose had given me the perfect cover for exiting.

"You're welcome," the cat purred.

I still needed to talk to Cookie alone, even if the scene in the kitchen wasn't the right time. I was convinced she knew more than she was letting on about what had happened to the Skeleton Trio and how much trouble they had been getting up to when they were smashed. As luck would have it, she was an equal opportunity stresser-outer, so there was no way she had told Grant anything to help his investigation, any more than she had told me.

Taking Lark and Pep with me, I went to sit out by the cauldron and wait for my grandmother; she had to show up eventually The day was crisp and the air smelled like fall, and it didn't take long for Cookie to join us.

"That was a smooth exit if ever I saw one," she said.

"Thank you," I said.

"What is it you wanted to talk about?" she said.

"Were the Skeleton Trio stealing stuff from the house?" I asked.

"Of course they were," she said. "Didn't you see their smug expressions all the time?"

"No, it wasn't something I noticed," I said.

"Maybe if you lived here you would've done," said Cookie.

"Why didn't you tell anyone?" I said.

"No one asked," said Cookie. The wind blew leaves all around us.

"What exactly were they stealing?" Lark asked.

"I don't know," said Cookie. "You're lucky I'm answering your questions. Next time I want a bottle of wine for my trouble."

"Where did they keep all the loot?" Pep asked.

"I don't know that either," said Cookie.

"Are you lying?" I asked.

"Do not say, 'I don't know,'" Lark said through gritted teeth.

"I had an idea of where they were stashing it," she said.

"Why were they hiding things in the first place?" I asked.

"Because of Down Below! Everything that goes wrong here is because of Down Below," Cookie said.

"It doesn't seem like a lot has gone wrong until recently," Lark said. "Whereas Down Below started generations ago."

"You'd be surprised," said Cookie.

"Has somebody shut off your wine stash before?" Pep asked.

"Only Meg," she said bitterly.

"But you don't know where they were stashing the stuff they stole?" I asked again.

"I said I have an idea, but I don't really know. I'm not the one to ask," she said.

"Who is the one to ask?" Lark asked.

Unfortunately, she wasn't about to tell us. Mostly because at that very moment we heard a scream, and all four of us raced for the house, toward Audrey's voice.

Chapter Eighteen

We went running and skittering into the kitchen, because we knew Audrey wasn't one to be dramatic. If she was screaming, there really was something wrong.

"What is it?" I cried out.

Audrey didn't seem able to say a word, but she responded to my question by simply pointing outside.

Outside the window was a ghost, larger than any I had ever seen. He was solid, and parts of him were stamped with the mark of a skull, in red. Grant's mention of the Root of All Evil came to mind immediately, and I knew this appearance was no accident.

I wondered where the color had come from, but that wasn't the remarkable part of this vision. The remarkable part was that the ghost was slowly breaking apart another skeleton and tossing the bones onto the air to fall wherever they landed. As we all watched, horrified, the ghost turned toward us, waved slightly, and dropped the rest of the bones to the ground.

My mom and Meg went racing out the door. Grant, my brother, and my cousins were all away from the mansion, and so was Lizzie (three cheers). They were busy searching for whoever had done the smashing, but in the process they had left the house unattended.

In a crisis like this I could of course just wave my hand and do magic, but it might not necessarily work very well. Usually to go along with a spell there was a bit of noise or music, as my grandmother liked to call it.

It took years and years of practice to be a very good witch, so unfortunately Cookie was the best witch of all of us. She did have lots more practice under her belt, because as she liked to remind us all the time, she was old. She was also crazy.

With magic, a witch just had to say what she wanted and it would be true. There were no wands. Our ancestors thought wands were too much trouble, so the witches of old had practiced and practiced until wands were obsolete. Now it was just a wave of the hand and voila, magic.

I watched my mother and Meg waving frantically, but the ghost didn't seem to want to stick around and attack them. Magic sparked and boomed and fizzled before my eyes, but the ghost didn't intend to get hit. Instead it simply melted back into the darkness of the evening.

My mom and Meg were running, something I hadn't seen them do in a long time, but there was no way they were going to make it to the strange ghost before it disappeared.

"We going to help?" Lark asked.

"Leave it to me," said Cookie, her small eyes snapping left and right. She stepped past us before we could stop her.

"You get the feeling she's a lot more mobile and capable than we give her credit for?" I wondered.

"Daily," said Lark.

"It makes me nervous," said Pep.

"What should we do?" I asked Audrey. My aunt's hair was doing its best impression of a cactus.

"Our power will be minimal because we just had a full moon, but we should still be able to enact some kind of strong enchantment. Why don't you three start gathering herbs for protection and I'll start with some pure water."

Water-infused protection was one of our most basic enchantments, one that always worked well for the three of us. We rushed around the kitchen doing as Audrey asked, while she busied herself filling the largest pot with hot water and then hanging it over the crackling stove.

I glanced out the dark window from time to time but saw no sign of the ghost. My mother, Meg, and Cookie were still out there, leading me to wonder out loud, "Are they gathering up bones?"

"Probably," said Lark. "If we boil the remains we'll increase the enchantment for strength and protection."

"Won't the skeletons mind?" I said.

"Not if it helps keep them safer," said Pep.

After a few more minutes of frantic preparation on our part, my mom and Meg came in looking sweaty and tired. Cookie was holding the bones as if she was very proud of herself. She marched right up to the pot and plunked them in without asking, then turned to glare at Audrey. "You might have started it, but I'm the one who knows what we're doing. Don't look at me like that."

Audrey stopped looking at her like that.

"Where did the le-haunt go?" I asked.

"Back into the woods," said my mom. "But I have a feeling we'll see him again."

"What do you think of the red blood?" I asked.

"I think it was paint and he was trying to make himself look like a creep," said Mom. "Make sure everything is cleaned up for when the customers arrive."

"Are you okay, Mom?" Lark asked.

Meg gave a tired smile and laughed, "Happy birthday to me."

When everyone else came home, Cam, Corey, and Kip were furious that they had missed the fun. Grant was furious that we'd boiled the bones before he could complete an examination.

"We must be allowed to do our work," he fumed.

Sure, sure, was the look Cookie gave him.

She stuck her finger in her ear and wiggled.

The next morning at breakfast, everyone's concerns were aired out in an appropriate forum, meaning that there was lots of yelling, red faces, and hand-waving.

"Those bones were evidence," Grant cried, showing temper for the first time. "What if they were the key to solving this case?"

"We already know who did it," said Mom. "We know it's the Root of All Evil. It's just a matter of proving it and discovering their motivation."

"Our lives were in danger. We did the only thing we could do to save them," said Meg.

"Did you dump the water all around the mansion?" Grant asked tiredly.

"Of course we did. How else would it work as a protective measure?" my mom asked. "This is a business. We can't have the Root of All Evil attacking skeletons; they're part of the haunted house."

"They're going to keep attacking unless I complete this investigation successfully, and the only way I'm going to do that is with your cooperation, which I'm not getting," Grant said, setting his jaw stubbornly.

"You'll solve it, don't worry," Cookie said, patting his hand comfortingly.

I watched Grant get control of himself, and with an effort he managed to calm down a little. He was usually so quiet and reserved that his outburst made me realize that he really cared about solving the case, it wasn't just a job to him.

"Can you please show me exactly where the ghost was?" he asked, returning to his usually polite tone.

"I sure can," said Cookie cheerily. "Anything to make you happy."

"I highly doubt that," Lark muttered.

"It was really stupid of you," said Lizzie. "You should've waited for us to get back."

"You think we can't take care of ourselves?" Lark asked.

My brother, Kip, and Corey winced, knowing that Lizzie shouldn't have been so critical. Lizzie, as usual, either didn't realize it or didn't care. And in any case, she wasn't the only one ready to get on our case.

"I'm not so sure you *can* take care of yourselves against an opponent like this. You may not understand how dangerous he is," Kip lectured.

"I may not understand what? I actually saw that ghost out the window," Lark insisted, "and you didn't. I can take care of myself just fine, thank you very much. We're perfectly capable witches, and the fact that we're not out there on patrol like you lot doesn't mean we couldn't be."

"No need to be so sensitive," said Lizzie.

"I'm sensitive like a rock," Pep retorted.

"Nerves of steel," grinned Lark. "You should know how it feels. That's what your head's made of."

Lizzie threw down her napkin and pushed her chair back quickly and loudly, her face whitening. "Fine. Don't take my advice. I'm only trying to help." She tossed her luxurious hair over her shoulder and stormed out of the room.

"You just had to bait her?" Corey asked.

"How did you get so good at it?" Cam asked.

"It just comes naturally," said Lark.

"I've been practicing for a long time," said Pep.

Now it was my turn to push my chair back. This weekend was Meg's party, and the grand opening of the season for our

SpookyBooSpectacular. Either event alone would have meant a lot of pressure and a lot of work; having them come right on top of each other was almost more daunting than I could contemplate. Having guests on a regular night was one thing, but the SpookyBooSpectacular would at least double the number of customers we'd have flowing in and out of the haunted house.

I wondered how much was going to go wrong.

Knowing this family, a lot.

I tried to focus on the finishing touches we were working on for the grand opening, but with the smell of cake permeating the house I could barely concentrate for wanting to go eat chocolate.

"This is going to be the best-looking SpookyBooSpectacular ever. All of us put so much work into it," said Lark.

We planned to release several owls that night, so I knew Rose would go into hiding—she had threatened to retreat to my room—because owls were dangerous to cats. There were also going to be extra bats on hand, and we had all the ghosts and skeletons we'd need.

We would all be in costume, and Meg and Audrey would take turns minding the gift shop. Since Pep was younger, it made more sense that she should do the hard work of managing the haunted house while they could sit behind a counter and sell goods.

"How many people are coming to the SpookyBooSpectacular?" I asked.

"Lots," said Lark. "I heard the Chief of Investigators telling someone at the market that they were going to patrol, just in case. They think most of the bed and breakfasts around here are going to be full of people coming to enjoy the event. It's going to be crazy."

"We have to go all out with the costumes," said Pep.

"We just have to be careful not to become part of the haunted house ourselves," said Meg, coming up to us with a smile.

"Do you remember a couple of years ago when the SpookyBooSpectacular went totally wrong?" Pep said.

"How can we forget that?" said Lark.

I shook my head. "I must have been when I was still in college."

"Oh, it was a whole to-do at the time. It was these two guys in their twenties who got stressed out when they saw the vampires. They freaked out and somehow managed to escape Cam, who was leading their group through the haunted house. They thought it was such a good haunted house that they tried to become part of it and scare people themselves. Needless to say, the supernaturals weren't happy about that development."

"That's ridiculous," I said. "Did you get to them before the vampires did?"

"Yeah, but barely," said Pep, shivering.

"They were confused about why we seemed to think it was a life or death matter. I don't think they realized that their lives were at stake. Literally."

"Did you explain it to them?" I asked.

"Mom tried, but it's not as if they had any idea what was really going on," said Lark.

"That's just as well, obviously," I said. "Shall we do the hay bales next?"

We spent the afternoon rolling hay bales out of the barn and pulling them into bits to scatter over the lawn. Then we added more fake gravestones and cobwebs. After that we tried to come up with a good excuse to go into the kitchen, but Audrey wasn't having it.

"The smell of cake is so strong I can't stand it," Pep moaned. "How long until dinner?"

Audrey went over to the kitchen sink to wash something as we were about to leave. "That's funny," she said.

"What?" I asked, turning back.

"There doesn't appear to be any hot water," she said.

Pep, Lark, and I spread out to different bathrooms and tried various faucets, but there was no hot water in any of them.

"We'll have to fix this on the double," said Pep as we reconvened in the cheery kitchen.

But just then the sound of yelling split the air. The three of us exchanged looks and Lark said, with a little smirk of satisfaction," Lizzie must be trying to shower."

"So, we can wait a little while to fix it," I said, grinning. "But what could have happened to the hot water?"

"A couple of things," said Audrey. She was making bread. The counter was covered in flour and she was using the dough to clean it up as she talked. "It could be something wrong with the pipes, which would probably be serious, or maybe something went wrong with the boiler, which might be easier to fix."

"Where's the boiler?" Lark asked.

Audrey hesitated and Pep said, "In the basement."

My heart started to thump faster and harder.

"You'll need to get your mother," said Audrey, who had gone back to cooking, not to be deterred for long. "She'll know best how to handle this."

"Okay, I'll get her," said Lark, heading outside.

Meg and my mother were working on the grounds, feverishly trying to get all the decorations in place.

"I'll go with you," said Pep to Lark. They she turned to look over her shoulder at me. "Hold the fort till we get back?"

Part of me whispered that I shouldn't go looking for trouble, but another part was saying I should go down to the basement myself and get some answers. And this was the perfect opportunity; I even had an excuse. The Down Below crowd couldn't possibly be angry if the boiler was broken and one of us had to come fix it. We couldn't very well expect them to do it for us.

My mind raced, trying to think of an excuse for not getting Mom. But before I could think of anything plausible, I saw something blond marching across the backyard.

"Lizzie's already on it," said Lark.

"She looks like a wet rat," I said.

"She couldn't finish her shower," said Pep as the four of us stared out the window.

Given how immense our property was and how busy Meg and my mom were, it would take Lizzie a long time to find them, which left us a little window of time to do what we had to do.

"We should get back to work," I said.

Audrey should have been suspicious of my tone, but she was too busy making sure her bread was rising properly and just nodded absently without looking up.

I glanced up at one of the cabinets and saw a pair of blue eyes looking down on me. It was Rose, surveying the room, and I had the distinct impression that she was shaking her head directly at me. She wasn't supposed to be in the kitchen in the first place, and Audrey had no idea she was there, so I shook my head back at the white animal in return.

Lark saw where my eyes were going and snorted. Rose was sitting above the stove on a shelf that held a variety of boxes, and she wasn't easy to spot. It was also the warmest spot in the kitchen, a feature which, coupled with the delicious aromas, explained her presence there.

Crazy cat.

Carefully, so as not to draw Audrey's attention and have her order us to stay away from Down Below, we left the kitchen.

Someone had to go to the basement, and that someone was me.

Chapter Nineteen

We didn't waste any time, above all because the hot water was off and that wasn't good, even when it wasn't winter. Fall was still cold in Maine, and Uncle Taft needed his warm bath, not to mention Cookie and the rest of us. Cookie had enough temper to keep her steaming for hours, but I knew that if I waited to go Down Below, my brother or Kip or even Grant would come and stop me. My mother also wouldn't be pleased. None of us had been Down Below in years, and for good reason.

"This is NOT a good idea," said Pep, staring at the basement door.

She stood on my left while Lark flanked my right, for all the world as if they were my bodyguards.

Which they weren't.

"We need to go down there," I said firmly. "Something is going on here, and it doesn't bode well. And I have a feeling it's all emanating from Down Below."

"You really think so?" Lark asked.

"Where else could it be coming from?" I said. "They're lawless down there, and they have no use for us. My best guess is that they want to drive us out and take over the haunted house for themselves."

I had long suspected something like that, and the attacks on the skeletons were only strengthening my hunch.

"The Root of All Evil are in our own basement?" Pep whispered.

"As close as they can be," I said grimly.

"We're going with you," said Lark firmly.

"No way," I shook my head. "There's no reason all three of us should risk our necks."

"Staying here is just as risky for us," Lark pointed out. "If your mom comes back and finds out we let you go, she'll never forgive us."

"Yeah, she'll probably stick us in one of the coffins," said Pep with a shudder.

There was a long trail of stories about the coffins being one of Cookie's favorite punishments for her children when they were younger. I wasn't sure any of us really believed the stories, but we also didn't want to take the chance.

"Maybe we should just hold off for a couple of days and do a tactical analysis," Pep suggested.

"You're kidding, right?" Lark scoffed.

"We need to plan and prepare. We can't just run in there and hope for the best," Pep argued.

"Sure we can! We're about to," said Lark. "You can't go without us, that's all," she insisted, looking at me. "No way you get to have all the fun."

I sighed. "All right, you can come, but we have to go now."

"Right," said Lark.

Pep shifted nervously.

None of us moved.

"It's not going to open by osmosis," said Harold.

All three of us jumped.

Harold was a le-haunt who had joined us less then a year ago. He loved all things circus- and theater-related, the performance, the attention, and everything else that came with being part of the haunted house. He was kind and funny and loved the mansion. My mom thought he'd been a real find.

"You're encouraging us?" I asked, glancing between him and the firmly closed door.

"Not officially. Lark is right, your mom is scary, but something has to be done. All of us here at the house are worried, and if anyone is going to solve this mystery, it's going to be you three, not some outsider."

Was that a veiled insult directed toward Grant? Or maybe not so veiled?

"Are you sucking up to us?" Lark asked.

"Most definitely," Harold confirmed. "Is it working?"

"Kind of, yeah," Lark laughed.

"Have you been down there?" I asked.

Harold shuddered. "Certainly not. You think I want to risk my neck?"

"Comforting," said Pep. "I think this is a terrible idea, but I don't see any way around it."

"Always so positive," Lark muttered, running her fingers through her short, dark curls. "Let's get this over with."

With that she marched forward and grabbed the doorknob, but just as she took hold of it, something moved in the corner of my eye.

We had an audience. Several le-haunts, ghosts, and skeletons had come to see us off. They all looked like they were going to a funeral, and since they'd all attended their own, I felt like that was saying something.

"We're going to be fine," said Pep. But her face was white.

"Good luck," whispered Harold.

Steve had turned up as well, and he waved goodbye as if he was never going to see us again.

Lark stepped forward, grabbed the door handle again, and pulled. At first nothing happened, but then the old white door swung open and a burst of warm air hit us squarely in the face. The basement was warm, at least that was something. I hated creepy, cold basements.

"Let's go," I said, glancing back at our send-off party. "We'll be back soon."

I tried not to look at any of the faces too closely as I said it, because I knew none of them believed me.

We were just about to close the door behind us when there was a scuffling sound.

"Wait, take this," Harold said, reaching out with a torch that looked like it was several hundred years old. It was ornate and metal and bits of it were starting to rust.

At first I recoiled in surprise. "Where did you find that?" I asked.

"It's what was on hand," he said.

I shook my head. Of course.

I took the torch and examined it. At least the lighter in the middle looked new. Harold reached out with a match and lit it, and the next instant warmth was covering my face.

"Now you're ready," said Harold.

"You really think we'd ever be ready?" I asked.

"I strive for positivity," said Harold. "Way to ruin it."

I gave him a small smile and turned away. Lark and Pep were still standing at the top of the stairs, neither looking inclined to go forward. All I could see beyond them was blackness.

My cousins parted slightly so that I could walk between them. As the one with the light, I was going first.

Down Below had already been taken over by the time I was born and growing up, so I had never once been in my own home's basement. Stories of danger abounded. Now we were going to find out whether they were true.

The stairs were surprisingly wide, crafted of a plain wood and covered in a layer of dust that revealed the markings of footsteps. That someone had climbed up to the door, and recently, fit with the fact that I had seen the *Spooky Times* beneath the door.

With a gentle current of air blowing upward, the snap of the door closing behind us didn't surprise me at all. I knew that Harold wasn't going to lock us down there, but I still listened for the turn of the bolt. When it didn't come, I was relieved. I knew several of the ghosts and skeletons would wait for us to return—if we managed to return at all.

"Are you sure about this?" Pep whispered.

"Not at all," I said.

We moved down the stairs with care. I kept looking at my foot before taking a step to make sure I wasn't going to land on something gross, but the stairs were clear of anything that might have tripped us up. The walls on either side were made of stone, and there were small chinks missing where water had dripped through. The foundation was made of large slabs of stone that looked melted together, but that I knew had just formed a smooth surface in the long years since the mansion had been built.

"I'm surprised there isn't a large welcoming committee," Lark muttered.

"You think they heard the door?" Pep asked nervously. Her voice echoed off the walls.

"I'm sure they did," I said. "There probably isn't a guard because it's been so long since anyone came down here, so what would they be afraid of, anyway?"

"If you asked Lizzie, she'd say they should be afraid of His Majesty of Magic," Lark rolled her eyes.

"I still don't think he's real. Grant is probably just lying because he likes the attention," I said.

Next to me, Pep was silent.

Moving downward felt like forever, but it really didn't take that long.

I was expecting a dirt floor when we reached the bottom of the stairs, but instead we found layers of rugs. I supposed I shouldn't have been surprised about that, either. Before Down Below was created the basement had been used for storage, and there had probably been a large selection of rugs to spread around.

I examined the layers, but I saw nothing out of the ordinary.

"I keep expecting something to jump out at us, or blood to drip from the walls," Lark said.

"I actually think it's quite nice so far," said Pep. The place was warm and nicely carpeted and clean, which at this point was more than you could say for the rest of the mansion. We were in a small space that was kind of like an entry hall, and there were doorways to our right and left, but no doors.

There were also no lights in either direction, but I could hear noises from the left. Since the basement entrance was on the right side of the mansion, most of the space was to the left, so it didn't surprise me that this was where a gathering was taking place. I also heard the churning of a machine, maybe (I thought) the *Spooky Times* printing press.

The breeze was stronger now, and the flame guttered but held. My heart skipped a little. If the flame went out we'd be entirely in darkness, and I didn't care how pleasant Pep thought this place was, there was no part of me that wanted to be down here without a light.

"To the left we go," said Lark.

We were just about to pass through the doorway when a shadow stepped in front of us and we stumbled to a halt.

"Just where do you think you're going?" a skeleton in a topcoat asked, brandishing a long sword.

We had found Down Below. Whether that was a good thing or not remained to be seen.

Chapter Twenty

We had dealt with any number of skeletons over the years, but this one looked especially old.

How does a skeleton look old, you wonder?

Well, newer skeletons' bones are whiter and cleaner. Older skeletons show the wear and tear of time passing by the color of the bones, which get darker and more brittle-looking as the years go by.

This skeleton had the dirtiest-looking bones I had ever seen. Whenever he moved they creaked, and he was moving right now because he was swinging his longsword.

"What are you doing with that thing?" Pep demanded.

The skeleton stopped moving. "What do you mean?" he asked, taken aback by the challenge from such a small human. Pep had that effect on, well, skeletons.

"That's an important historical artifact you're swinging around willy-nilly. You can't just be walking around with it," Pep said.

"But it looks cool," the skeleton argued.

"You better take care of it," said Pep.

"I will," the skeleton assured her, looking confused.

"Fudgy Bail?" I said.

The skeleton sputtered but regained his composure quickly.

"You can't just prance down here and see Fudgy," the skeleton replied.

"Why not?" Pep asked.

The skeleton opened his mouth to reply, then closed it again. He obviously didn't know why not either.

"Well, because you've never been here before," he said at last.

"There's a first time for everything. What does that have to do with anything?" Pep demanded.

"There's a protocol for such things," he said after another pause.

"How can there be a protocol if it's never happened before?" Pep said.

"It's not as if a human has never come down here before," said the skeleton.

"We aren't humans, we're witches," I said.

"Oh, right, okay." The skeleton was getting more confused by the minute.

"Who else has come down here, anyway?" I asked.

The skeleton clammed up at that, realizing he had said too much.

As we waited for an answer, Pep crossed her arms over her chest and started tapping her foot impatiently, which clearly made the skeleton even more uncomfortable.

"Oh, very well," he said with exasperation, and turned back the way he came. He narrowly missed bumping the sword into one of the stone walls and quickly glanced at Pep to see her giving him a dark look.

I hadn't gone one step before I realized that Down Below really started through this doorway. The clanging of the press was louder, as was the laughter.

"This is going to be interesting," Lark said.

On either side of us were little rooms with open doorways. The walls in each room were covered with designs, and in front of those were piles of furniture.

"Do you ever wonder if one of our ancestors collected antiques?" Lark asked.

"I have a feeling it was Lady Oakley," I said.

"That makes SO much sense," said Pep.

As we passed the nooks and hollowed out spaces, skeletons, ghosts, and one or two le-haunts came to peer around unfinished door frames to stare at us. They looked different from their counterparts upstairs. These supernaturals were less chirpy, and they wore clothing that was darker but otherwise nicer than what the ghosts who worked at the haunted house wore. These supernaturals didn't have appearances to keep up, so they dressed in fine garments. Down Below was not what I expected at all.

"You think he was referring to humans who've been down here recently?" I whispered to my cousins.

"I have a feeling it was Cookie. If there's trouble, she's always close by," said Pep quietly.

"Maybe it was your mom," Lark suggested. "There has to be a reason why we've gotten along so well with Down Below all these years. I have a feeling we've been told stories as kids to try to scare us, but the reality is different."

I thought about that. My mom had been coming down here on a regular basis my whole life? I supposed it was possible, but the idea certainly required a re-examination of my impressions of the last couple of decades.

"Right this way," said the skeleton.

When we reached what I thought was the end of the basement, the skeleton started bowing toward the doorway to our right. Dim light filtered through it, and next to the doorframe the skeleton indicated a sconce where I could leave my torch while we went inside.

I could hear laughter and the clink of glasses. There was definitely merriment in progress.

"This place gets stranger and stranger," said Lark.

I glanced behind us to see the countless doorways stretching back down the hall. In each one, several ghosts and skeletons were peering out at us. When I looked at them, their heads quickly disappeared.

"They're so nosy," sniffed the skeleton. "I'm Peter, by the way."

"Nice to meet you," said Pep. She introduced each of us in turn, and as Peter stretched out his bony hand, each of us took it and shook it gently. I felt like I was shaking claws, but it clearly made him happy.

From inside the room a booming voice called, "Stop distracting our guests and let them in. It isn't every day we get a visit from witches."

Looking a little sour about having his new friends taken away, Peter nodded and walked past us. As we were going through the doorway he said to someone in the hallway, "I know! It's very exciting that we have visitors! I can't wait to tell you the story."

The three of us exchanged looks and smiled. Peter apparently also liked gossip.

I don't know what I was expecting when I walked into this last space, but a card table with two skeletons, two ghosts, a vampire, and a le-haunt was not it.

At the head of the table sat one ghost, larger than the other ghosts and wearing several layers of gold chains around his neck. A cigar dangled from his mouth. When he saw us he set down his hand of cards.

"Well, well, well, if it isn't a Garbo herself," he said, leaning back and puffing.

"Sorry for disturbing you," I said. My eyes moved nervously from right to left. If we were in danger it would be now.

"No disruption at all. We love guests here," said the ghost, his voice booming and jovial. "I'm Fudgy Bail."

"Jane Garbo, and these are my cousins, Pep and Lark," I said.

"These are my associates," said Fudgy, nodding toward the other supernaturals at the table. They were all dressed splendidly, each wearing some sort of large jewel. They set down their cards while they waited for us to continue our conversation, and it was only now that I saw what they were playing with: gold coins. I wondered if they were real.

"What can I do for you?" Fudgy asked. The only light in the room came from a dim lamp in the corner, perfectly placed to cast a shadow over Fudgy's face and make him seem all the more intimidating.

"There have been some mishaps upstairs," I started slowly.

"You mean the Skeleton Trio and the other attacks?" he asked.

"So you know," I said. A haze of smoke filled the room, tickling my throat and making my eyes water.

He and his associates all chuckled. "Of course we know. What goes on upstairs directly affects downstairs. We keep tabs on all sorts of things. I knew when you came back and I knew things would be different from then on," he said.

"How will they be different?" I asked, wondering how my presence figured into any of this.

"Times are changing," he said, as if that explained everything. "I suppose you came down here because you think the trouble is coming from Down Below?" He didn't sound angry at the implication, but I knew I still had to tread lightly.

"I thought it was a possibility," I acknowledged, feeling that it was best to be honest.

"I'm glad you came down," he said.

"Why?" I asked.

"Because it gives me a chance to tell you directly that nobody from Down Below has anything to do with what's going on upstairs," he said. "I would never allow it. We have a good thing going here and there's no reason to ruin it."

"It would be difficult for us to get upstairs without detection given that there's just the one door," added one of his associates. The light flickered over his face and I found his facial expression hard to read.

"That's true," said Pep.

"Is there anything you can tell us that might be helpful?" Lark asked.

Fudgy Bail paused for so long that I thought he might not have heard the question, but eventually he spoke.

"The trading of information is very important," he said. "Some might say it is sacred. Down Below we have our own set of rules and our own way of doing things, but I can tell you this, everyone knows how important information is."

We waited, knowing what was coming.

"What I mean by that is that maybe I have some information, but why should I give it to you?" he asked.

Lark was about to reply when Pep cut her off. "Because whatever is going on upstairs, even if it doesn't have anything to do with you now, it's only a matter of time. Whoever is smashing up skeletons will eventually come Down Below. For all we know, that's the ultimate goal of the whole campaign."

The ghost turned his old eyes on my smart friend and smiled. "Maybe it will come here and maybe it won't. Still, I'm very good at making deals. I wouldn't be in the position I hold if I didn't know that there's always a deal to be made. And I'm less afraid of what may come than you might think."

Pep stepped forward, her eyes intense. "The skeletons were smashed, completely smashed. There was nothing left of them."

Some of the associates shifted uncomfortably and glanced at their leader, but his face remained impassive.

"There is no reason for me to help you. Trouble has not come here and it may never," he said.

"So you do know something?" Pep prompted.

He briefly closed his eyes, visibly annoyed. When he opened them he leaned forward and said, "I know everything you know."

"What is that?" Lark asked.

The ghost gave a thin smile. "I know that the trouble did not originate from Down Below."

Recognizing that we weren't going to get anything more out of him, we took our leave, but not without mentioning the problem with the water heater.

"Of course you can fix it. It's much better than your mother having to come down here," he said.

"Thank you for your time."

Peter offered to show us where the boiler room was, which meant leading us through another labyrinth of small rooms with low ceilings and lots of supernaturals staring at us as we passed.

The passages were dimly lit, and it was hard to see any distance ahead. Off the main hallway, the rooms were colder and the draft more biting.

"It's not often that we get visitors down here," said Peter cheerfully.

"Aren't you bored?" Lark asked.

"Oh, never. It's impossible to be bored when there are so many laws to be broken," Peter chirped.

"Why didn't I think of that?" said Lark.

"I don't know, but if you keep coming down here your heart will surely blacken. Then again, at least you still have a heart," the skeleton finished thoughtfully.

"Three cheers for that," said Lark dryly.

"Here it is." The skeleton paused before a wide, sturdy-looking metal door.

"You expect us to go in there?" Pep asked, staring at the door as if it were a snake about to bite.

Peter, who had clearly decided that Pep was worth pleasing, looked concerned. "You asked to be shown where the boiler room was and I brought you."

"If we asked you to steal something for us, would you do that too?" I asked.

"Oh, no, I only do something like that for pay," said Peter.

"But you'll do a favor for free?" Pep asked.

"Only once," said Peter. "Besides, I expect that you owe me now."

"Of course we do," I said.

"Lark and I will fix the heater. Pep, can you stay out here?" I said.

"I sure can," said Pep. She looked at the skeleton, who gave her a big grin.

"You want me to teach you how to pick pockets?" he asked excitedly.

"Maybe next time," said Pep.

Lark and I opened the heavy iron door.

I held the torch aloft, banishing the black interior. Inside was your standard boiler room, only more so. This was, in fact, the largest boiler room I had ever seen, also the oldest.

We walked over to examine the boiler and saw something very interesting. "Look, the little lever has been switched. That's the only problem," said Lark in amazement.

"But doesn't it take somebody physically moving the lever to turn it off?" I asked.

She glanced at me and nodded. "Yes, it does."

Both of us stared into the shadows for a minute, thinking about what that meant. "So, somebody wanted us to have to come down here," I said finally.

"That's about the gist of it," said Lark.

"Now the only question is, are they friend or foe?" I said.

Lark looked at me grimly. "I think that all depends on whether we make it out of here."

We switched the lever back so the mansion would have hot water again, then headed back to Pep.

"Not to be too much of a worrywart, but let's get out of here," said Lark.

I couldn't have agreed more.

Without wasting any time, we went back out to the dark hallway where we'd left Pep. Since we had taken the torch, she had pulled a lighter from her pocket so she could see. As we emerged from the boiler room she quickly flicked the lighter closed and stuffed some cards into Peter's hand. He then stuffed them into the pocket of his dress suit, trying to look as innocent as possible and failing miserably.

"Having fun, are we?" Lark asked.

"Oh, sure," said Pep.

"What were you doing?" I asked.

"I was just learning some card tricks," Pep said defensively.

"If she ever decides to turn to a life of crime, watch out," said Peter. "She's a natural."

"We need to get out of here. Now," said Lark.

Peter pouted. "But I haven't had time to show you how to hot-wire a car."

"That will have to be next week's lesson," said Lark. "Can you please take us back to the stairwell now?"

Grumbling about how little fun we were, Peter nevertheless did as we asked.

I felt my unease growing with every step we took. Unlike before, when there had been countless skeletons and ghosts watching our progress, now the dark doorways were empty. No faces peered out at us this time.

I wondered where they'd gone to, even though I knew I might not like the answer. Our footsteps echoed dully off the walls, and with each flicker of the fire in my hand I thought someone was coming toward us or moving away.

"Is it just me, or is this place too quiet?" Pep asked out of the side of her mouth.

"Gee, I don't know, why don't you ask your new buddy?" said Lark.

"You're just jealous because I got to learn something new," said Pep.

"I'm not jealous that you're learning how to turn to a life of crime," grumbled Lark, her voice equally low. We all felt that if we spoke any louder, we'd remind the supernaturals that we were Down Below, and we didn't want to do that.

"I really don't see what the big deal is. I like learning new things," said Pep in a whisper.

"What's that noise?" Peter asked, peering down one hallway and then the next.

"Are we almost to the stairs yet?" I asked, with a sinking feeling in the pit of my stomach.

"Yes, I think so," said Peter, but his voice had started to shake. "Isn't it getting louder?"

"It sounds like a lot of running feet," said Lark.

"How is that possible?" said Pep.

"Is that what it is?" I asked.

I looked at Peter, but he wasn't looking at me. He had frozen in place and was staring down one of the dark hallways.

"How fast are you three?" he whispered, staring straight ahead.

"We aren't going to win any races, but we aren't slow," said Lark. "I could outrun these two if my life depended on it."

"You could not," said Pep. "I'm clearly the smallest *and* the fastest."

"I would stop arguing about it and start doing it," said Peter.

"Why?" I asked, but I had a feeling I already knew.

Peter lifted a shaking hand and pointed down the dark hallway. At first I didn't see anything, but when my eyes adjusted to the darkness I noticed a flickering and realized that the noise was getting louder fast.

Finally it came home to me that what we were hearing was the sound of skeletons running.

Many skeletons.

And I could also see ghosts flashing through the air.

"What are they running for?" Pep asked.

Peter turned ominously toward her and said, "You."

"We'd better get a move on," said Lark, starting forward. "Are the stairs that way?"

Peter was pointing ahead of us, which was the direction toward which the skeletons were also running. In order to make our getaway, we'd have to beat them to the stairs and get up them and through the basement door before they caught us. We had hardly any time left.

"It sounds like hundreds of them," said Pep.

"That sounds about accurate," said Peter nervously.

"What are you talking about?" Lark asked. "Everybody seemed so friendly."

"But we didn't actually think you'd come down here. How foolish would you have to be to come Down Below? We just moved the lever as a joke, thinking we'd get a complaint, but then you three show up in person." He said the last bit as if he couldn't quite believe it.

"You lured us down here as joke?" Lark cried.

"We didn't think it would be you three who actually came," Peter whined. "We thought maybe that handsome warlock would come or something. That would have been nice."

"What handsome warlock? The only one here is Grant." Lark sniggered at her own joke, in part because it was so clear how ridiculously good-looking Grant was and in part because she made bad jokes when she was stressed.

"And now all the ghosts and skeletons and le-haunts are angry at us . . . why?" I demanded, glancing again down the hallway.

"Why not?" said Peter meekly.

"This is getting us nowhere, and anyhow, we have to get out of here," I said.

We didn't waste any more time. Without so much as a goodbye to Peter, the three of us dashed forward. I watched my arms pump and thought how strange it was to be running madly in my own basement; I had never been much of a runner.

I could see the stairway ahead and to the right, and beyond that I could see skeletons pounding down the long hallway.

They were coming. We didn't have much time left.

Chapter Twenty-One

"Get up the stairs," Lark cried, pushing her sister and me in front of her so she could bring up the rear. Pep stumbled on the first step but righted herself, looking around wild-eyed.

"They're coming!" Lark cried.

We took the stairs two at a time; they surely hadn't felt this long when we came down. I was still holding the torch, mostly in case we needed it as a weapon. I could see a very thin sliver of light across the bottom of the door as we got close to safety.

"Open the door," Pep yelled.

"Now I have you," I heard someone yell from behind Lark.

I looked back to see a skeleton reaching out for her and Lark stopping to try and defend herself.

"No," I yelled.

Without thinking I spun around and took several steps in one leap. In the darkness I lifted the torch and swung it at the skeleton, who immediately backed off, looking surprised.

"Run," I yelled. I took one more swing for good measure and then turned and raced back up the stairs.

"Open the door," Pep bellowed again.

This time whoever was on the other side of the door must have heard her, because the sliver of light widened and the door swung away from us.

"Just a couple more steps," Lark cried.

As the three of us tumbled through the door, I took one backwards glance. A mob of skeletons crowded the stairs, but they had paused when the light from the doorway reached them. They didn't want to come into daylight any more than we wanted them to.

The three of us went tumbling through the door and landed one on top of the other. I heard a jumble of voices and a slamming of the door behind us. Breathing hard, I tried to get my bearings.

What I saw when I finally looked up was the very angry eyes of my mother. Shaking a little, I broke eye contact and glanced around.

Meg was giving her own daughters an unbelievable glare, but thankfully the rest of the family was nowhere in sight, nor was there any sign of Grant.

"Kitchen. Now," my mother snapped.

Even the le-haunts were cowering.

My mother had an office, but it was so tiny we couldn't all fit inside it. When we had to have meetings where she needed to yell at us *en masse*, she always chose the kitchen. The location was great when someone else was in trouble, because the kitchen was easy to eavesdrop on, but it was disheartening when it was you getting a scolding. I didn't want to think about Lizzie with her ear pressed to the other side of door, even though I knew that's where she'd be.

Miserably we walked past Grant on our way to the kitchen. His face was tight and his arms were folded over his broad chest. I had the distinct impression that he wasn't happy.

Lark, Pep, my mom, Meg, and I filed into Audrey's domain. The woman herself had said we could use the space while she took a break from birthday preparations. I didn't know where my brother and the other guys had gotten to, but I was relieved that they hadn't seen Mom greeting us as we left Down Below.

Lizzie had at least had the good sense not to ask if she could come for this little chat, but just as we were settling in around the island the door swung open again and Cookie walked in.

"This doesn't concern you," said my mom imperiously.

"Everything here concerns me," Cookie countered. "Besides, they're my granddaughters."

"You've tried to disown them at least seven times," said my mother.

"And has it worked?" Cookie demanded.

"Oh, very well," said Mom.

"Just what do you think you were doing down there?" she cried as soon as Cookie had joined us at the island.

"The boiler was shut off," I said.

"We had to find out if we could fix it," said Pep.

"You really think we're fools?" Meg demanded. "You really think we were never young witches in a mansion full of criminals and spooks?"

"Is this one of those times we shouldn't answer a question honestly?" Lark asked.

"Whoever said there are times like that?" my mom asked sharply.

"Cookie," all three of us chorused.

Meg shook her head and looked at Cookie, who merely shrugged.

"I would tell you the truth, but now you won't believe me," she said sadly.

"You can't be sneaking Down Below. It's not safe," said my mom. "Anything could've happened to you. In fact, I'm shocked you made it out alive."

"What would we do if something happened to you?" Meg asked.

"No one wants to hear your answer," said my mom to Cookie.

Lark, Pep, and I hung our heads.

"We're sorry," said Pep. "We really just wanted help. I didn't think anything bad would come of it."

"You had to run out of there," said my mom.

"There was bit of a misunderstanding," I said.

"Don't tell me you had a fight with Bail or something," said Meg, closing her eyes in consternation.

"We didn't," said Lark.

The relief in the room was palpable.

"How do you know about Bail?" Pep asked.

"You don't think someone just lives in our basement and runs a crime ring right below us and we don't know anything about him, do you?" said my mom.

"Then why didn't you ask him about the smashing and the Skeleton Trio?" I asked.

"That's none of your business," said my mother. She didn't bother to point out that even if she had made inquiries, she didn't have to report the fact to me.

"What is our business is how you decided to go down there in the first place," said Meg sternly.

"We're sorry," said Lark.

"I'm afraid sorry isn't going to cut it this time," said my mom.

I exchanged looks with my cousins. What were they getting at?

"Are you going to punish us?" Pep asked, looking nervous. "I've never been punished for anything before."

Lark snorted.

"Given that it's our opening weekend, we really can't have anything go wrong. You're to stay completely away from Down Below and completely away from this investigation! Do you hear me?" my mom barked.

"That is a rather light punishment, don't you think?" said Cookie.

"They're adult women in their twenties! What would you expect me to do?" said Mom.

"Kick them out of the mansion, at the very least," said Cookie. "Preferably, tell them they can never come back, but at a minimum kick them out."

"Who wants to check on the bats and ravens?" Meg asked, pointedly ignoring Cookie.

"Not us," said Lark.

Meg smiled evilly, and we all frowned. The ravens and bats were mostly left to their own devices, but they did have to be checked on from time to time, especially before the SpookyBooSpectacular. Usually one of the guys did it, because none of us wanted to go anywhere near the cave in back of the mansion.

But Meg was making her intentions clear. If we stepped out of line, we would be the ones taking care of the creepy creatures cave.

"We hear you," we said in unison.

My mom nodded that she was satisfied. "Now, we have a lot of work to do, so let's get to it so we can relax a bit before the customers arrive. The first thing we're going to get to is that I want you to tell me exactly what happened Down Below and exactly what you did, and I want you to tell me now."

I told my mom what had happened with Fudgy Bail and that we had fixed the water heater. I didn't mention that it looked like it had been intentionally turned off, justifying that by telling myself I couldn't be sure it was true, and it would do no good to speculate.

"Mr. Bail wasn't mad?" my mom asked.

"No, he seemed more amused than anything else," I said. "He didn't think the Root of All Evil were coming from the basement to attack haunted house skeletons."

"As well he shouldn't," said my mom.

"What makes you say that?" I asked quickly.

For a split second I didn't think she was going to answer, but then she said, "It's not really their brand of criminal behavior."

"Anything else?" Meg asked.

The three of us shook our heads. I left out the bit at the end where a group of supernaturals had chased us up the stairs.

Finally it was over. I could tell because my mother relaxed her grim face and asked Meg, "Are you ready to have the best birthday party ever?"

Meg rolled her eyes but didn't argue. "At least there will be delicious cake," she muttered.

That's what I was thinking as well.

I had calmed down enough by now to start processing what had happened Down Below. I didn't understand what Bail had told us, but he had obviously thought he was telling us something. The question was: what?

"The Root of All Evil is here. The end is coming. And today is our last chance!" Uncle Taft came yelling through the kitchen.

"Uncle Taft, nothing is wrong," said Lark soothingly.

"No, you don't understand, everything is wrong," he gasped.

He strode over to us, his hand resting on the sword at his hip, his eyeglass firmly in place, and his shoulder blades held tightly back. "You have to get out of here! You have to go now. You can't fight it, you can't stop it. The end is near," he cried.

"What makes you think the end is near?" Cookie asked.

My grandmother could find Uncle Taft completely exasperating, but she always treated him with respect when he had one of his fits. Maybe she recognized a kindred spirit.

For his part, he turned to her and looked relieved that someone sounded like they believed him. In fact, he looked like he was counting on it. "The clocks, obviously," he said.

"Whatever are they doing?" said Cookie.

"They're spelling doom," he cried.

"Is that doom with two o's?" my mom asked.

"You shouldn't encourage him," said Meg.

"I don't think he needs any encouragement," said Lark.

"Now is not the time to be arguing with me, young lady," said her mother. Lark quickly closed her mouth.

"It's okay, Uncle Taft. I'll take you upstairs," I said.

"Not until I check the grounds. Might as well keep them out while we still can. Don't worry, I have supplies for the expedition. I won't fail," he said.

With that he marched toward the back door and disappeared into the gray evening light.

"We've delayed dinner long enough, we might as well eat," said my mom, catching the sound of my stomach rumbling.

There was no part of me that wanted to face my family at dinner given that we had just been ordered to stay away from the investigation and everyone had surely been listening in. But I did it anyway. As I expected, Kip and Corey, my brother, Grant, and Audrey were all sitting around the dinner table. They had started eating without us, which was a small blessing. Maybe they would leave quickly.

Corey had just been saying something about the case as we walked in. He glanced nervously at us and then took a big bite of food.

"Just say it," said Cam. "They'll find out one way or another anyway. They're nosy like that." He glared at us.

I sat down and tried to act as neutral as possible so Corey would keep talking. If he had information about the case, I wanted to hear it.

We looked at my mom to see if she would object, but she knew very well that while she could order us to stop investigating, that there was no way she could keep us from hearing the information that was being passed around the mansion.

"I was only saying that my experiments were very interesting. I've determined that given the way the skeleton fragments were distributed, they weren't smashed where we thought they were," Corey explained.

"They were smashed somewhere else and then moved?" my mom asked.

"Quite so," said Corey. "I'm not sure where, though. And I can't think of a reason why anyone would do that."

"Can you?" my mom asked Grant.

The warlock shook his head. "Maybe to make it impossible for us to tell where the violence actually took place. That makes it harder for us to investigate who did it. It seems likely that if we knew where the real the crime scene was, it would lead us to the killer."

"Does this mean it was planned, or that the fragments were swept up?" I asked.

For a split second I didn't think anyone would answer, then Grant of all people said, "It would make more sense if the Skeleton Trio was explicitly targeted, but we just don't know."

As a matter of fact, I had assumed that the Skeleton Trio had been targeted because of the artifacts they'd been stealing. They had stolen something, then run into another supernatural doing something nefarious.

That had been my working theory, but now I wondered whether I was wrong. Could the motive have been something entirely different, that none of us had guessed yet?

Cookie was uncharacteristically quiet throughout dinner, and she excused herself early, saying that we had a horrendous party to prepare for and she needed to brace up for it by getting a good night's sleep.

"Who is she kidding? She doesn't sleep," Pep muttered as she, Lark, and I left the kitchen.

"Should we follow her into a stash of wine something?" Lark asked.

"I don't think so," I said. "I think we should get to bed as well. I have a feeling this weekend is going to be really busy."

"Our family thinks that's going to be in a good way," said Pep.

"We can't even get any more helpful information about Down Below," said Lark.

"Actually, they confirmed our worst fears," I said quietly.

Dinner was over, and we were making our way up the several flights of stairs to our rooms. Soon Lark and Pep would veer off to theirs while I continued the climb to the attic. We were snatching these last moments before sleep to talk about the case.

"What do you mean?" Lark asked.

"What he said confirmed that the smashers weren't from Down Below. His point was that whatever part of the Root of All

Evil is on this property, they're right here in the haunted house," I said.

Chapter **Twenty-Two**

Unlike the woman herself, Meg's birthday party was a subdued affair. She was only having the party in the first place to appease her mother-in-law; as far as she was concerned, the less fuss the better.

Thank goodness Audrey made such good cake.

We had spent the day in frantic preparation for the opening extravaganza.

My mother had been loath to cut off work early, but she had insisted that everybody shower and look nice for the party. On top of that, many of the ghosts, vampires, skeletons, and other creatures would be attending Meg's celebration.

We usually gathered in the kitchen for parties, but this time we were using the Great Hall. This was a room that had probably once been great, but as Lark said, it stopped being great when people stopped going inside it on a regular basis. We had no use for such a large room anymore except for occasions like tonight.

Cookie took credit for the whole thing, of course. She showed up dressed in so many sparkles, it was hard to look directly at her.

For some totally unknown reason, I was very nervous about the evening. I had changed outfits a solid six times, each of which required me to run down to the unused bathroom on the floor below to check my appearance in the mirror. Lady Oakley suggested that I bring one of the old standup mirrors in from the other side of the attic, but I ignored the idea just because she was the one who had come up with it. Still, I made a mental note to do it the next day.

In the end I landed on a black dress with a black cardigan and comfortable shoes. Given that this was just a family affair, the evening didn't really call for anything crazy. I also put on an old beaded necklace that I loved, which had belonged to my great-grandmother. It added a bit of pop to my outfit.

I decided to leave my hair down and flowing, which I usually didn't do. Mostly it was the ponytail for me, because who has the time for that fancier sort of thing?

Feeling good about myself at last, I had headed downstairs to meet up with Lark and Pep. I was excited to see them, so when I walked into Lizzie instead my disappointment was considerable.

"Oh, hey," she said, as if she'd never seen me before.

I had thought I looked good until Lizzie looked me up and down with a little smile on her face. She was wearing a metallic dress with spaghetti straps. It was so short . . . well, it was just very short.

I tried to maneuver around her without actually having a conversation, but she wouldn't allow it.

"You look nice. Homey," she said.

"I didn't think Meg would want us to wear anything that was too too crazy," I said, trying not to look her up and down in return. As usual she looked like she belonged at a club in the city and not in the middle of nowhere in Maine, going to her aunt's slapdash birthday celebration.

"Yeah, that's why I put on something old and didn't put much thought into it," she said offhandedly.

My eyes narrowed. She was hiding something. "Are you excited for the party?" I asked.

"I sure am. I hope there's dancing," she said. "Maybe Grant will ask me to dance and we'll start things off together," she added, her eyes taking on a dreamy expression.

So there it was. She wanted to look nice for Grant. I shouldn't have been surprised.

"Anyway, I wanted to do one more check in the mirror, so I'd better be going. I don't want to miss the entrance of the cake," she said, proceeding to waddle up the stairs. Her skirt was so tight she had trouble lifting her leg on each step. I turned around so she wouldn't see me sniggering.

"There you are," said Lark, coming out of her and Pep's room. Her black hair was tightly curled on top of her head and she was wearing a black leather jacket and black jeans. She had put what looked like dog collars on her wrists and ended up looking like she belonged in some sort of biker chick gang. I guess everybody looked like they belonged somewhere else.

Pep followed close behind her sister, looking much more normal. She was wearing a blue skirt and a white blouse with a blue cardigan, plus delicate gold earrings for good measure. Her hair cascaded everywhere as usual, but she had at least tried to clip some of it back along her temples. She looked very cute. In short, very Pep-like.

"This is going to be fun," said Lark. "Was that Lizzie I saw leaving? I don't suppose it was permanently?"

"Yeah, just to check her makeup again," I said. "Where is everybody else?"

"I think they're already in the Great Hall," said Pep.

"How is your mom taking it?" I asked as we made our way to the party. Already I could hear music and laughter, and the air was filled with the most delicious smells.

"The fact that we're having a party in her honor?" Lark asked.

"She's upset about it," said Pep. "I don't know why. She does so much for the family she *should* be celebrated."

"Good evening, ladies," said Mirrorz, who had materialized at our elbow as he so often did. The man was as silent as a vampire, which he was.

"You look nice today," said Pep.

Mirrorz was turned out in his best coat and tails. Vampires were always very well put together, but Mirrorz especially so, and tonight he was looking extra elegant even by his own high standards.

"Thank you very much," he said, smiling briefly. "I must get back to the kitchen and supervise."

As he strode away Lark said, "Those are some nice white gloves he has."

We had entered the Great Hall as we talked, and it looked splendid.

"These are some decorations," Lark marveled.

"I think it's something Mom threw together," I said.

Mom had kicked us all out earlier in the day and performed some sort of magic that we weren't supposed to know about. The result was that the Great Room was decorated in sparkling banners that read "Happy Birthday Meg," and that it was clean and swept, which it certainly had not been that morning.

"Don't give her all the credit. I helped," said Cookie, appearing in front of us with a big smile. "How do you like my outfit?" she asked, striking a pose.

"You look like you're a variety show performer from the sixties," said Lark.

"And who's to say I wasn't?" said Cookie.

"Explains all the drama," said Pep quietly to me.

I laughed. "Let's go," I said.

I led the way to a table where a plentiful array of finger foods was spread out. We filled our plates eagerly and went to a quiet corner by the fire to chat.

There were ghosts, le-haunts, and vampires everywhere, but no skeletons yet. The le-haunts were attempting to put on a show that mostly involved making guests move away from them and protect their glasses of champagne.

"This is fun," said Cam, who showed up in a coat, but with no tie. His hair was slicked awkwardly back and he smiled at us.

"It's a great time," I said dryly.

"Who are the people we don't know?" I asked.

"They're a handful of other witch friends," said Pep. "Mom doesn't think they came for her, she thinks they came to see the mansion and mingle with the vampires, but who knows. I told her that everyone likes her and she shouldn't be surprised if they want to celebrate her birthday."

"Very true," I said, surveying the room.

"Look at the woman of the hour," Gus called out. He was wearing a bowtie that looked like it was choking him as he floated around dreamily amongst various groups of ghosts.

Aunt Meg walked in with my mom and Audrey, a big blush on her face. Instantly Cookie started clapping and pointing, "Birthday girl! Birthday girl!"

"Thanks for coming, everyone" said Meg. "The cake should be out soon."

"Cakes," Audrey corrected.

The middle generation of my family split up and started to mingle. My mother and Meg immediately zeroed in on a couple of the visiting witches, and in short order they had all moved to a corner and started whispering. I was desperately curious to know whether they were talking about the events with the Skeleton Trio, but I knew I couldn't find out without drawing my mother's wrath down on my head.

Despite the fun and laughter, I was uneasy. We hadn't caught whoever had smashed the Trio, and tomorrow was SpookyBooSpectacular, the season's grand opening extravaganza. We needed everything to run perfectly, and with the attacker on the loose the chances of that happening seemed small.

As my thoughts swirled, I sighed and examined my glass, but there were no answers there. I knew I was missing something, and I was sure it was something that should have been obvious.

But my attention was soon drawn back to the party. It didn't take long for demands for cake to become overwhelming, so Audrey returned to the kitchen and reappeared a few minutes later pushing a cart laden with a large cake. Behind her was Mirrorz, pushing another cart with two more cakes.

Applause rang out around the room.

"Where are the skeletons?" Pep asked suddenly. I hadn't seen any sign of them, mostly because after the cake arrived I'd gotten distracted by the need to keep an eye on Grant. I shrugged and told her they were probably just fashionably late.

"How's that going, by the way?" Lark asked, nodding in the warlock's direction.

"How's what going?" I asked, clearing my throat.

"Staring," said Lark.

"I wasn't staring," I said.

"Oh, please. What color is your mother wearing tonight?" she asked.

My mother was now standing behind me, but I had been facing her when she walked in. I had no idea. "Black?"

"Gray," said Lark. "See what I mean?"

"I just like watching Lizzie make a fool of herself," I said, knowing that all three of us knew I was lying.

"Right, let's talk about the skeletons," said Lark.

"I don't know where they are, but now that you mention it, I don't like that they're not here yet," I said.

"You couldn't possibly think that all the other skeletons were in on smashing the Trio, could you?" Pep asked.

"You mean the Root of All Evil is comprised of the other skeletons? No, I highly doubt that," I said. I was sure that at least some of the skeletons were good.

"So where are they?" Lark asked.

"Oh. I think I found them," said Pep.

Without any more warning than that remark, the double doors opened to reveal every skeleton that lived at the haunted house.

The Great Hall went entirely silent. Even Cookie, who had been laughing uproariously at nothing, quieted down.

My mom and Meg were still in the corner speaking quietly with the other witches, but when the skeletons made their entrance they paused their conversation to watch.

The skeletons marched grim-faced (if a skeleton can be said to make faces) toward the center of the room, the ghosts, le-haunts, and vampires hurriedly moving out of their way.

"I demand to know why you're having a party when the Skeleton Trio's killers haven't been caught!" said the skeleton in the lead.

Everyone in the hall leaned forward, trying to listen. My mother's face was hard, but I couldn't hear her response.

I glanced at Grant to see how he was taking the intrusion, but he was simply looking on quietly. The man was maddeningly calm. I hadn't thought it possible that anyone could stay calm in the face of Cookie trying to ruffle him, but Grant managed it.

"We're doing the best we can. We have extra patrols, and nothing else of significance has happened," my mother assured him. I noticed her jaw tighten, though Grant didn't, and if he had, he wouldn't have understood what it implied.

I, on the other hand, knew her well enough to recognize when she was lying.

My mind flashed back to the incident where the solid ghost smashed another skeleton outside the window. She probably thought that was just some odd anomaly.

It was a good thing I hadn't told her about the little back wing incident where I had been attacked.

The skeletons had fanned out by now, and I wondered if they were trying to appear threatening. Given how many witches were in the room, I doubted it. Cookie, who had been acting silly a moment before, straightened up and looked serious. I wondered if she had really had as much wine as she pretended. Maybe she was dumping it in the base of the cactus plant when no one was looking.

The skeletons waited. One of them had gone to stand in front of my mother, and when I looked more closely I realized that this skeleton was the union representative. My mother obviously represented the Garbo family.

For a few breaths nothing happened, and I wondered what my mother would do. Then she reached out her hand to shake the skeleton's. He took it. An audible sigh of relief went up around the room.

At least for now, the haunted house supernaturals were on my mom's side.

But for how long?

It took me until late in the evening to realize that Uncle Taft was missing.

When I finally noticed his absence, I asked Pep and Lark, "Where's Uncle Taft?"

Pep looked around. She hadn't missed him any more than I had, but once she'd scanned the large, crowded room, she didn't see him either. "I don't know. Probably manning the battlements or something."

"Does that mean he's sleeping?" Lark asked.

"It's as likely an option as any," I said.

Our concern about Uncle Taft was sidetracked by the arrival of Grant in our corner, a glass of dark liquid in one hand and a cookie in the other. Looking rather happy, he strolled up and said, "Evening, ladies."

"Hi there," said Lark. "What do you think of the party?"

"I thought the entrance of the skeletons was exciting," he said.

"One wouldn't want to be dull," said Pep.

"One thing this place hasn't been is dull," said Grant.

"Have you had a lot of mysteries to investigate before this?" Lark asked.

Grant was settling in to chat with us, having finally torn himself away from Lizzie. She had watched him walk toward us with a mixture of anger and confusion on her face, but now she was drowning her sorrows by chatting with a good-looking vampire.

"I've had a few. There's a lot of training to go through before you can become a full-fledged investigator. For warlocks who are doing investigative work," he explained, "they don't want us to screw up and they want to minimize the danger we're in at all times."

"Isn't it hard to minimize the danger you're in when you're chasing criminals?" Pep asked.

Grant nodded. "We do our best, but obviously there's always an element of risk."

"Has anyone close to you died?" Pep asked.

"Pep, you can't just ask stuff like that," said Lark.

"Sorry," Pep mumbled. Sometimes she was so curious about the academic question on her mind that she forgot about the people behind it.

"It's all right," said Grant. "Obviously in our line of work accidents happen. A couple of my friends have died fighting supernaturals."

"That's awful," said Pep.

Lark and I agreed.

We stood silently for a while, surveying the scene in front of us as we thought about Grant's experiences. We watched witches chatting with vampires, skeletons talking to other skeletons, and everyone keeping a careful eye on the le-haunts in case they got up to any mischief.

Everyone in my family was there except Uncle Taft; even Cookie was walking around delightedly taking glasses of wine and downing them. But the majority of the attendees were supernaturals who worked at the haunted house. Usually the house was open on Friday night, but we had skipped tonight both because of the party and in preparation for the SpookyBooSpectacular.

"Have you made any more progress on the case?" I asked Grant.

His eyes narrowed, then he smiled. "I think knowing that the bodies came from elsewhere is progress. As to who did it, no, we haven't figured that out yet. When we do, I'm sure you'll hear about it."

"I'm sure you will soon," said Pep.

"Let's hope so," said Grant.

Suddenly there was a noise like a clinking of glasses. We looked around and saw my mother gathering everyone's attention by tapping her spoon on her goblet.

"If you don't mind, I'd like everyone's attention for a minute," she said. "As all of you know, Meg is as beloved as a sister to me, and I want to thank everyone for coming out tonight in honor of her birthday. The weather is supposed to be horrible starting pretty soon, so I also want to make sure to offer birthday wishes and appreciation out loud before our guests start to depart."

I glanced out the window to see a gentle patterning of rain already coming down. My mother had been worried about the rain all week, and now the prediction for the next day was for storms. Uncle Taft had warned that it would be the last night we ever saw.

"And now if everyone would join me in singing happy birthday," my mom said.

And everyone did.

The rest of the night went by quickly, mostly because there wasn't much of it left. People did start to leave early, and most of the supernaturals scattered. We all had a lot to do the next day and everyone knew it. Meg herself was just as happy to see the evening end. She did, however, sample every kind of cake. To Audrey's delight, she declared them all delicious.

I wandered away from the conversations and toward the big dark windows. If I went all the way up to the top of the mansion, where we'd found Uncle Taft the other day, I could see to the village on a clear night. Sometimes I enjoyed going up there and watching the small town life come alive in the dusky evening. There was something calming about having a normal village nearby, when there was nothing normal about the mansion at all.

The skeletons had settled into a subtle silence for most of the party, standing off in a corner. Their anger had subsided somewhat by the time the party ended, mostly because Cookie had gone over and started chattering at them. I think they developed some sympathy for my family after that.

After we finished cleaning up, everyone departed for their own rooms. But I wasn't tired, so I set off to wander by myself around the sweeping hallways and spooky rooms of the mansion.

Uncle Taft hadn't made an appearance all evening, and I thought I'd run into him in my wanderings, but every space I went into was quiet and deserted. My mind was mulling over the case of the Skeleton Trio, wondering if it had been the Root of All Evil that had attacked them, or maybe someone motivated by a personal vendetta. Had the attack had something to do with the stuff they were stealing from the mansion, or had it been entirely unrelated?

I couldn't be sure, but I was starting to think that the Skeleton Trio had been killed because they'd discovered something that someone else didn't want them to know. Maybe they got in the way of a crime in progress, but I doubted it. If someone wanted to steal something from the mansion they could have done it at any time over the last several decades.

No, I had a feeling that the Skeleton Trio had been in the process of taking something when they'd gotten in the way of a very nasty gang.

They had paid a high price. The only question now was, what was the Root of All Evil going to do next?

Chapter Twenty-Three

After I got tired of wandering through the house, I trudged up to bed at last. It was on nights like tonight that I really missed my old room on the fourth floor, the one that Lizzie had stolen. Just one floor down, but it felt like a world away.

It took me a very long time to fall asleep that night. I kept worrying about the supernaturals and wondering what would happen in the morning.

At first I thought someone was rubbing my face with a fluffy duster, although that would have been strange since I was pretty sure there was no duster in the entire mansion.

"Get off, Cam," I groaned. "Aren't you too old for his foolishness?" I tried to push my little brother away so I could fall back to sleep. When the duster continued to tickle my nose, I carefully cracked one eye open.

"So you're the culprit," I said groggily.

Rose was sitting on my chest, wearing a frilly white nightgown and swatting at my nose with one white paw.

"Be careful," I warned her, trying to sound dangerous. You can never be sure with a cat.

"I'm not going to hurt you," said Rose. "It's just fun."

"Is there something I can help you with?" I yawned.

For a moment Rose rested on my chest, causing me to cough slightly as she made her way to my shoulder and plunked down again. Now her furry side was in my cheek and she started nuzzling my jaw.

I reached my hand up to pet her head and the purring in my ear sounded like an engine starting up.

"You just wanted to get petted in the morning, didn't you?" I said.

"I figured you could have some company going down to breakfast. I know you tend to get lost on the way," said Rose evilly.

I rolled my eyes. "That was one time. You're just hoping you can have some bacon this morning."

"Maybe," Rose acknowledged. "Fried mouse would also be acceptable."

"Gross. Is that really what you came all the way up here for?" I asked.

"No, that is not what I came all the way up here for. I came up to yell at you for going Down Below without me," she explained, licking her chops. "Can you imagine how many mice there are down there?"

"I don't imagine Fudgy Bail would appreciate you killing his mice," I said.

"Does he think he owns the mice, too?" Rose asked incredulously.

"He thinks he's a good businessman, and good businessmen don't give anything away for free," I said, thinking back to his comment about information. He thought he was telling me something vital and important by saying that the Root of All Evil isn't in the basement, and I figured he'd expect an even trade sooner or later.

"You look pensive," said Rose. "It's not a look I've seen on you before."

"Very funny," I said. "Get off my shoulder. I have to get dressed."

Rose moved just enough so I could sit up, then curled into the warm spot I had left, her back against my pillow and her eyes half closing.

"Do you think the Root of All Evil is part of the team that works at the haunted house?" I asked the cat.

She gave me that judgmental look that cats wear and said, "It's the most likely explanation. Where else could they be?"

She had a point. "They could still be Down Below. Fudgy Bail could have been lying to us."

"He could have been. Maybe he was trying to protect his own, but his associate did point out that they would have a hard time sneaking out of the basement without being caught."

There was also the *Spooky Times* to consider. The newspaper bulletin had made it sound like they had no idea what had happened to the Skeleton Trio. It was just possible that only a couple of those supernaturals who resided in the depths of the mansion were responsible for the attack and the rest were in the dark.

Fudgy had insisted that he knew what went on in his domain, therefore he'd know if any of the Down Below crowd had done it. He had said they hadn't. Could I believe him?

I really didn't like the alternative.

I had thought I was going to be early to breakfast because of Rose, but I was wrong. By the time I made it to the kitchen, only Lark, Pep, and Cookie were still around. Everyone else had eaten and gone. Even Audrey wasn't there.

"Morning," I said. Cookie was standing at the counter pouring a cup of coffee, while Lark and Pep sat at the island polishing off muffins.

I went over to get some coffee just as Cookie poured the last of the batch into her mug, leaving none for me. She pretended not to notice and went to sit down, while I got a fresh pot brewing.

"Where is everyone?" I asked as I started to make more.

"The investigators are making a last-ditch effort to find the Root of All Evil," Cookie explained. "Everyone else is working on last-minute preparations for tonight. We're open an hour longer than usual, opening early, so we're very busy," she added as if we didn't know it, taking a sip of coffee and smacking her lips in appreciation.

"You look busy," said Pep.

"I'm old," said Cookie.

"You don't seem it," said Lark.

"I don't act it, either," said Cookie.

"Are you going to be at your cauldron tonight?" I asked her.

"Of course I am. How will I discourage people from coming otherwise?" said Cookie. "But right now we have to talk about this case. Where is that foolish white cat?"

"Rose isn't allowed in the kitchen," I said.

"Poppycock," scoffed Cookie. "She comes in here all the time."

Just then a white head popped up from her usual place near the stove.

"Someone not named Audrey call me?"

"Yes, come down here," my grandmother ordered, pointing one gnarled hand at the floor.

I hurried over to help Rose, but she jumped down from the cabinets in one swift motion before I could even get close. I gave a frightened cry in case she'd hurt herself, but she landed gracefully on the floor. I glared at her.

"What, I'm a cat," she said.

"You know how many times your height that is?" I asked.

"Enough that you should be very impressed," she said, swishing her tail.

"Yeah, exactly," I said.

Once we'd gathered around the island, Rose on her own stool, my grandmother leaned forward and said, "So what do you know about this case?"

"We didn't think you cared about this case," said Lark. "We aren't officially allowed to investigate it."

"Yes, yes, yes, stop wasting my time!" Cookie snapped. "I heard you all getting scolded just like the rest of the mansion heard. You and I both know you're investigating even if you're not supposed to be. It's the Garbo way. Now tell me what you know while we still have a few minutes."

The three of us looked at each other in wonder.

"What's she doing here?" Pep pointed to Rose, who was looking very interested.

"Why wouldn't you want the smartest and brightest to help?" asked Rose, sounding confused.

"You mean the smartest and brightest cat?" said Lark. She wasn't a big fan of the furry animals, though she didn't dislike them as much as Audrey did.

"No," said Rose.

"She's here to help," said Cookie with finality. "She can go places we can't and observe stuff we don't. I mean, you three don't observe much of anything, but that's beside the point."

"Okay, we'll start from the beginning, just stop insulting us," said Lark.

"We can't help it," said Rose.

"It's a sign of affection," Cookie grumbled.

"Be less affectionate then," said Lark.

We spent the better part of the next hour filling Cookie in on our investigation. At first her face remained impassive, but as time wore on she started to look more alarmed. It was the longest period of time I had ever seen Cookie pay attention to a single topic and not say anything sarcastic. That made me think she was really taking this seriously.

Cookie licked her lips as we talked, and her eyes shone brightly.

"What about the Root of All Evil?" I asked her. "Are they just a myth?"

Now my grandmother looked grim. "They aren't a myth I've ever heard of before, but I imagine they're real enough."

"Why do you think they smashed the Trio?" I said.

Cookie shook her head. "Certainly not because the Trio represented all that was kind and good in the magical world." She paused for a moment, thinking, then went on. "I would say your guess is as good as mine, but the truth is, it's probably better. The Trio broke rules and were annoying. Those rules were in place for a reason, especially the one about not going out at night. Not all ghosts and vampires are warm and fuzzy creatures. Some are very dangerous. They appear fun and entertaining at the haunted house, but in real life things are different."

"They are all dead, after all," Pep murmured.

Cookie's head bobbed. "Exactly."

"So you believe that the Root of All Evil aren't Down Below?" I said.

"I don't know about that. Old Bail has plenty of reasons to lie," she said.

"Like he wants to deal with it himself?" said Lark.

"That or maybe he's part of it, or the simplest explanation of all, he just likes lying," said Cookie.

"Don't know anyone like that," Lark murmured.

"What about what smashed them? We haven't found anything big enough to do it," I said.

"You didn't find anything big enough on the grounds, but now thanks to Corey we know that they weren't smashed on the grounds," said Cookie. She kept glancing over her shoulder and out the windows as if she very much expected my mother or Meg to walk in and start ordering us to get to work.

It was a real concern.

"There are tons of things in the house," I mused. "Any of the heavier furniture would do. There's so much, we may never figure it out."

"Mom's coming," Lark hissed.

"We should try to figure it out, though" said Cookie quickly. "Everything might depend on it."

For once, she was serious.

After that ominous conversation, we got to work. It did occur to me that Cookie might just be messing with us, that she enjoyed pulling our chain, so to speak.

But she really did seem to believe that the members of the Root of All Evil (what is this, a cartoon?) were a dangerous lot, and anything that threatened Cookie's family (besides Cookie herself) had to be dealt with harshly. I decided to take her at her word for the moment, and concentrate on the tasks at hand.

"Stringing up fake cobwebs is actually one of my favorite jobs," said Pep.

We were in the topmost floor of the haunted house, where a large circular window overlooked the front driveway. Through it we could see Cookie mixing ingredients into her cauldron.

Today she was surrounded by three black cats who liked to roam the property. Rose didn't like them and they didn't like her, and once that had been agreed upon they mostly stayed away from each other.

Cookie offered one of the cats something she was holding in her hand. The animal sniffed it, shook its head, and trotted further away.

"This is my favorite room in the whole house," said Lark, slinging her fishtail over her shoulder.

The last room in the haunted house before you started descending stairs again was a library. Books would fly out at you, flung by whichever ghost was assigned the room that night. You'd hear howling, and at just the right moments bats would flash past the large window, though with rain coming, that was less likely to happen tonight.

We had been working in the haunted library for an hour or so when we heard footsteps on the stairs, and a moment later Cam appeared. "Lunch. Mom wants everyone to come so we can discuss finishing touches for tonight. She doesn't think we'll have time for a proper dinner."

Audrey didn't usually help out at the haunted house except on nights like tonight, when refreshments were sold and served. She wouldn't have time to cook a meal for the family, so it would be cold sandwiches for us.

The three of us put up the last cobweb and headed after Cam, taking the stairs two at a time. Meg was waiting for us when we reached the kitchen.

"Eat up," she said.

There was a massive pot of spaghetti on the stove, and we got in line to fill our plates. The kitchen was about twenty degrees hotter than the rest of the drafty old house, but all I cared about was that my stomach was rumbling and we weren't anywhere near done with the prep work.

Grant wasn't there, and it wasn't until we were all seated that I heard him enter the kitchen from behind where I was sitting. He came into my line of sight a moment later, walking quickly and looking serious. Rain was coming down harder now, lashing at the windows, and I'd heard several cracks of thunder.

"Is everything okay?" my mom asked him, noting his expression.

"Warlocks are coming tonight," he said. "We need all the help we can get."

The table fell silent.

Then a twitch drew my eyes to Lizzie. Her blond hair fell perfectly straight down her back and she was dressed all in black leather. I could just see her bouncing in her chair.

Anticipation hung in the air.

What now?

"I hope you won't be too angry that I called them," he said to my mom. "Whatever is about to take place will surely take place tonight. The Trio ended up smashed for a reason, and I'm afraid that whatever that reason was, we need to get to the bottom of it and make sure this family is protected."

"Of course. No, I think it's good," said Mom, to the surprise of all of us. She noted our expressions and scoffed. "I'm not totally unreasonable, you know."

"Could have fooled me," said Cookie, searching for the nearest bottle of wine.

Mom grabbed it and snaked it away from the older woman.

"See," Cookie grumbled.

Another moment stretched out before the silence was broken again.

"Is His Majesty of Magic coming tonight?" said Lizzie.

The boys perked up, while Grant continued to eat his spaghetti.

"No, he's not coming tonight," said Grant. "The warlocks who are coming are very capable."

Lizzie slumped back in her chair, disappointment personified. Then she straightened and asked, "Did you know there's a rumor that he has the most perfect warlock numbers and percentages?"

"No one cares," said Lark.

"Are they as good as Pep's?" Cam asked.

"Better," said Lizzie.

"You'll be pleased," said Grant. After a beat I realized that he was speaking to me.

"About what?" I asked.

"That His Majesty isn't coming," he said. He was smiling, but I had no idea why.

"I can't say that I care one way or the other," I said. "We don't need him to solve this mystery."

"He would be SO helpful!" cried Lizzie. "How can you say that! Can you imagine? It would be great."

I took a big bite of spaghetti and regretted it the moment I realized that Grant was still watching me closely.

"When will the warlocks arrive?" my mom asked.

"Soon. The weather is slowing them down, but they're on their way," he explained.

"I don't suppose they want costumes?" said Meg. "We have a whole dressing room filled with them. So many trunks I've lost track."

Grant laughed. "Probably not."

"Worth a shot," said Meg. "I suppose they'll look pretty intimidating in their ordinary getup anyhow."

A large clap of thunder interrupted the conversation, and for a quiet moment we all stared out the window at the rain. It was now coming down in thick gray sheets, so heavily that the barn and the field behind us were invisible.

"Think people will still come for the opening?" Meg worried.

"Not as many. We're going to have to set Cookie up in a boat," said my mom.

"I'll get to work on it," said Cookie.

"You don't want one of us to do it?" Lark asked.

"Are you kidding me? You'd conjure a boat with holes in the bottom. I'd capsize," said Cookie.

"It's not as if it has to be seaworthy," said Lark.

"With this weather you never know," Cookie shot back.

"Excuse me?" Steve had come into the kitchen, something I'd never seen him do before. "We're all getting a little worried about the weather," he explained, glancing at the windows where the water was pinging against the panes.

"What about it?" said Mom.

Steve hesitated. "The ghosts."

"They'll be fine," she said, her jaw tight.

"Of course," he said. "The skeletons are ready. We're waiting in groups." He said it as if to remind Mom that everyone was worried about what had happened to the Trio, plus the lack of progress in solving the mystery.

"We've made progress," Cam said as Steve let the kitchen door shut behind him. "We know the Trio was killed outside and we know that the murderer is at the mansion."

"All comforting facts," I agreed.

Mom cut the discussion short. "We need to get back to work. There's a lot to do before tonight. Grant, if you wouldn't mind informing me when your colleagues get here?"

"Of course," he agreed. "I'll go look into where they are now."

Grant strode out of the room and the rest of us got back to work. As I was passing through the foyer I ran into Cookie, all decked out in yellow rain gear with, you guessed it, cookies all over it. Even her rain hat was in the shape of a witch's hat.

"Be careful," I told her, passing the grandfather clock, which had been cleaned since the last time I'd see it.

"Will do," she said. "I've been in worse."

As she opened the door I saw how hard the rain was coming down and found myself wondering if there even was worse than this.

Cookie was having none of the actual weather, though, and used an enchantment to create a canopy over her head, thus staying dry.

"What was the point of the rain gear?" I yelled after her.

"Makes me look cool," she cried over her shoulder.

I rolled my eyes and kept moving, heading for the gift shop. They needed extra merchandise ready to go because of the number of customers we expected tonight.

"Can you deal with those boxes over there?" said Pep as I came in. The lights were on and she was blasting pop music while she worked. Lark was nowhere to be found, having come up with an excuse to help Audrey re-paint one of the haunted house rooms instead.

I quickly started emptying boxes of trinkets for the display in the middle of the shop. From ghosts to vampires, all the supernaturals in the haunted house were represented.

Of course, the witches won the prize for the most trinkets. You had to represent all types of witches, tall and short, young and old, blond and brunette, even a few redheads to make Lark happy.

I was pulling trinkets out of boxes when I came across some miniature models of the whole haunted house. I held one up and examined the little black statue. Something was niggling at the back of my mind, but I couldn't think what it was, so I pulled another one out of the box and compared the two.

My breath caught. The grandfather clock had been dirty, now it was clean. Who had cleaned it? No one in the house dusted, ever. It wasn't a thing. When my mom cleaned she used magic. Besides, the rest of the foyer was still covered in a layer of dust, but not the clock.

Heart pounding, I leaped to my feet.

"I'll be right back," I called to Pep, who looked up in confusion as I dashed out of the room.

"Where are you going?" she yelled after me.

I dashed to the foyer, my heart racing. The grandfather clock stood there, shining.

My cousin ran up behind me and I felt her brush my elbow. "What is it?"

"It's the clock," I said, pointing. "I found the murder weapon."

Chapter Twenty-Four

There was a buzzing in my ears. A perfect moment of clarity overtook me. It all had to do with the clock face . . . The grandfather clock was a fixture in the hallway. My mom loved it, and therefore we knew it would never go anywhere. Cookie hated it and thought it was an eyesore, but even she knew better than to cross my mom about it. All the kids knew that playing and maybe breaking something were all well and good, but the one thing we should never risk breaking was the clock.

In short, it was my mother's most important possession.

"Wow," said Pep, echoing my own feelings.

I was stunned at the idea that the clock had been used as the weapon.

"That's why it was suddenly so dusty," I murmured.

Pep flinched a bit. "Gross."

"I just assumed everyone was too busy to clean it," I said.

"We *were* too busy. Running a house and a business ain't easy," said Pep.

"Magic must have been used," I replied. "There isn't a scratch on the clock, so it's not as if it was tipped over and went crashing to the floor."

"True, and I wonder why someone waited to clean it," said Pep.

"Probably because the family was always around," I said, thinking hard.

"Yeah, no matter how many times Meg asks her, Cookie refuses to move out," Pep said.

Ignoring Pep's joke, I asked myself who would have done this. Who *could* have done this?

Just then a figure passed outside the window, moving quickly. It wasn't Cookie, because she was all decked out in yellow, and this shape was almost as dark as the darkness behind it.

"Is that Grant?" I asked.

"Where's he going in such a hurry?" said Pep.

"I don't know."

"He's coming this way. Do we tell him what you figured out?"

"No way. He'll kick us out of here and turn it into a crime scene."

I raced forward, determined to at least have a look at the clock before Grant got there and ruined everything.

"Why do you think he's out in this weather, anyway? It's just crazy," said Pep.

"Cookie went out," I said absently.

"See what I mean? Crazy," said Pep.

The massive grandfather clock loomed over the foyer. I took a quick look behind it, but its back was flush against the wall; there was no space back there where anything could have been hidden.

Bracing my hands on one side of the tall clock, I tried to push it sideways. It didn't budge.

Pep came to help me and we tried again, but the clock still didn't move.

Then, just above my head, I thought I saw something that looked an awful lot like skeleton dust. I was reaching up to get a better look when I was interrupted.

The door burst open in a shower of wind and water. I leaped back from the clock, hoping my urgency would go unnoticed.

Water cascading off him, Grant came into the foyer. His eyes met mine and then slid to Pep, who was standing where I had left her.

"I know you miss me when I'm gone, but I really don't need a welcoming committee," he said.

"We weren't welcoming you," I scoffed, realizing my mistake too late.

The door shut behind Grant and he said, "Then what are you doing in the foyer?"

"We were just on the way to the gift shop," said Pep quickly.

"What were you doing outside?" I said.

"Checking the grounds," said Grant.

"In this weather?" I challenged him.

"Especially in this weather," he said.

The three of us stood silently for several seconds.

Then Grant pointed behind us, "Isn't the gift shop that way?"

"Yes." Pep started marching back the way we had just come. As she passed me she linked her arm with mine, dragging me along. "Inventory to take and schedules to make!"

Glancing back over my shoulder, I saw Grant watching us. I walked faster.

Had he realized that I was examining the clock? What had he really been doing outside?

Once we were safely inside Pep's domain, she shut the door and closed her eyes.

"Phew, that was close," she said.

"You can say that again. Do you think he knew what we were up to?" I asked.

"No way," she said. "We can't go back, though."

"We'll have to wait till tomorrow," I said.

I wasn't happy about it, but there was nothing else to be done. The foyer wasn't likely to be empty again tonight, not while the haunted house was open to the public.

"It's strange, don't you think the other warlocks should have gotten here by now?" I asked.

"Yes, I do," said Pep grimly.

We spent the rest of the afternoon in the gift shop. I tried to concentrate on the task at hand, because Pep would never forgive me if I didn't record the inventory accurately. But at last it was dinnertime.

There'd been no sign of anyone since we'd rushed back to the shop and shut the door. Cookie hadn't come to chat, no one had come to say that the visiting warlocks had arrived, and I hadn't heard a sound from the other side of the door except the occasional click-click of the skeletons' feet.

"This is the last box. I'm just going to leave it for now. Let's go to dinner," said Pep, putting the box of black cat stuffed animals behind the counter.

"Where's Mom?" I asked Audrey as we entered the kitchen. No one else was there. Even Audrey looked grim.

"She didn't have time to eat. Customers will be arriving in an hour. Grab something quickly and then come help me with the finishing touches on the haunted library."

The SpookyBooSpectacular was about to begin.

My feeling of foreboding only grew after our slapdash dinner. Everyone in the family was dashing around doing last-minute prep; only Grant stayed motionless, setting up shop in the foyer and staring out the window. The rain got ever heavier until it became almost impossible to see anything outdoors. Whenever I went through the main entryway Grant was there, his hands clasped behind his back and his eyes forward.

Finally, not long before the customers were due to start arriving, I passed through the foyer and he was gone. I stood, baffled, until Cam came tumbling in to say that the warlocks hadn't made it to the mansion.

Then Mom came in, frantic.

Grant showed up, deeply concerned.

Lizzie arrived, solicitous.

In light of the weather, the missing warlocks, and the unsolved crime, Mom had finally panicked. She didn't think opening night could go forward as planned, and now we were faced with the question of what to do next. With the wild weather, she didn't think many customers would be coming anyhow, but for good measure she asked Cam and Lizzie to make some kind of sign to put up at the end of the driveway.

Once Cam and Lizzie were on their way, I looked sharply at Mom and asked, "What now"?

Mom, however, was staring grimly out the same window that Grant had been gazing out of earlier, and before she could answer my question Grant said, "I have to go find my colleagues."

"In this weather?" Mom asked worriedly.

"They're stuck on the road," he said. "As of our last contact they were almost here, so they should have arrived long since. I have no way to communicate with them if I stay here, and if they're in trouble, as seems likely, they'll need my help. I'm sorry to leave the mansion, but I don't have any choice."

My mom nodded agreement. "You should take helpers with you," she decided.

Amazed that Grant didn't insist on going alone, I stepped forward and said, "I'll get my coat." I was relieved that I'd be able to do something useful at last.

"No, not you," said Mom.

My mom was stubbornly stubborn. Once she got an idea in her head, like the one that said her little girl couldn't hunt, she was almost impossible to budge.

I stopped dead. "I want to help," I told her.

"You can help by staying here," she said. "We can't leave the mansion deserted."

"Cookie and Uncle Taft are here," I said, about to burst from frustration.

"Exactly. Cookie can't be left to her own devices. She'd do as much damage as if we handed the mansion over to the Root of All Evil on a platter," said Mom.

"Your mom has a point. Someone needs to stay here," said Grant, looking intently at me. He was dressed all in black and his large-brimmed hat was tilted over his eyes. He looked dashing.

"This isn't any of your business," I fumed.

"Don't talk to company like that," Mom snapped.

It took great effort not to roll my eyes.

"Get Pep and Lark. You can all stay," she said. "We'll be back shortly."

"Even you're leaving?" I was incredulous. Mom never left.

"Like Grant said, they might need help. They were almost here when we last heard from them, so we won't shouldn't be gone long. And with customers warned that the SpookyBooSpectacular is postponed, there shouldn't be any problems here."

As if putting me completely and instantly out of her thoughts, she turned to Grant and said, "Gather the others. If we're going to help the warlocks we need to get to them as soon as possible."

Grant gave one curt nod. Without looking at me, he turned and left the foyer.

I was furious. As Mom went to make final preparations for their departure, I went in search of Mirrorz.

After looking for a long time, I found him dusting bookshelves in the library.

He looked surprised to see me and said so. "Everyone else is leaving. The warlocks are in trouble. I'm to stay at the mansion."

Mirrorz black eyes softened. "Your mother only wants what is best for you. Her only daughter is very important to her."

"I want to do something exciting! The action is out there where the warlocks are, not in here," I complained.

"Someone needs to stay and defend the mansion," said Mirrorz. "The supernaturals can't be left alone and defenseless."

"But why does it have to be me?" I fumed. "There have been no attacks since the Trio. There isn't even proof that whatever attacked them is still out there. Mom could just cast a spell."

"That isn't as strong a defense as having an actual witch," said Mirrorz. "You'll see. Your presence here is vital. Just you wait."

"There you are," said Lark, coming into the library with Pep right behind her.

"We heard the news," said Pep.

A crack of thunder split the air.

"They're leaving now," said Lark.

The three of us headed back to the foyer, where we found Corey, Kip, Cam, Grant, Mom, Meg, Audrey, and Lizzie all dressed in black rain gear. I couldn't believe they were all leaving; it was as if they had lost their collective mind.

Cookie had also come in, and when I turned around I was surprised to see that Mirrorz had followed us from the library.

"We'll be back in no time with the warlocks," said Lizzie. "Imagine, helping out real warlocks. It's the most exciting!"

"Don't worry about us. We'll be here drinking," Cookie waved lazily. She paused, then added, "Actually, maybe we'll go into Shimmerfield and gather some supplies. Be a dear and spread the word that Uncle Taft is in charge of the mansion, won't you?"

Mirrorz inclined his head.

"Are you sure leaving is wise?" I asked.

"No," said Cookie, grabbing my arm and marching me away from the group. "Put a lid on those protests," she said out of the side of her mouth.

"We can't leave," I told her.

"No, but Mirrorz is going to spread the word that we did," she said in a hushed tone.

I'd never seen Cookie sound this serious before.

"This is no time for messing around," I told her.

"I'm not messing around," said Cookie. "This is serious."

"You'll forgive me if I'm surprised that you realize that," I said.

"I never forgive," said Cookie.

"I thought not," I told her.

By this time, most of the family was walking out the door with Grant. I felt a pang when I saw him on his way looking so dashing, handsome, and determined.

Lizzie clung to one of his arms and simpered, "We just have to be brave."

He gently freed himself, but he continued to smile down at her.

My stomach flipped.

"Let's get a move on," my mom said. She had put on black parachute pants, army boots, and a cape. Meg and Audrey were dressed in much the same way, while Lizzie was outfitted in her usual leather. The boys had also all dressed alike, in black.

"Hold the fort," said Mom. "We'll be back before you know it."

Cookie gave her a crooked salute and my mom rolled her eyes.

"Be careful," said Pep, sounding worried.

"We will be," her mom assured her.

Corey pulled the front door open and a gust of wind and rain slammed into all of us. Shutting their eyes against the terrible weather, almost everyone I cared about, plus Grant, left the mansion. Cam brought up the rear and tried to close the door, but the wind was too strong. Grant had to turn around and help him pull it shut.

Once they were gone I stared at the puddle of water spreading across the floor.

"All right ladies," said Cookie, her whole demeanor changing. "Let's get to work."

"Really?" Pep was incredulous.

"I bought you some time to figure out who was behind the attack. Everyone is out of the house, but they'll be back, unfortunately. Let's get cracking."

Chapter Twenty-Five

"First," said Cookie, who seemed to have a complete plan in her head, "everyone split up. Pep, you look in the chest in the drawing room. Lark, I want you to look behind the third bookcase in the library. Jane, make for the second back pantry."

"We aren't gathering your wine for you," I said.

"Why not?" my grandmother grumbled.

"Because like you said, time is of the essence," I told her. "We have to find the Root of All Evil before the family gets back."

"Don't admit you're related to them," said Cookie.

"I don't usually admit I'm related to you, either," I said.

"Thatta girl," said Cookie.

A crack of lightning lit up the dim foyer and we all paused.

"Have you ever seen lightning that close?" Pep whispered.

"Sure I have," but even my grandmother sounded unsure. "Okay, we'll forget the wine for now."

"And do what?" Pep asked.

"Defend the mansion!" said Cookie grimly. "We have supplies to gather, and then we'll head for the gift shop. Do it quietly."

The four of us split up, and I was glad to see Rose come trotting up to walk with me. The whole place felt empty with most of the family having run off into the storm.

The ghosts, le-haunts, vampires, and skeletons were all hunkered down in their respective wings, preparing for the exciting evening ahead. I didn't have the heart to tell them the big event was postponed; they'd find out soon enough when everyone else came home.

"How are you doing?" Steve asked as I passed him.

"I've been better."

He nodded knowingly. "It's been a bad business. At least the warlocks are coming. It's very lucky we have such skilled help."

"Very lucky," I said, and kept moving so I wouldn't have to tell him that the warlocks were delayed.

"Jealous he's so impressed with the warlocks?" Rose asked as she trotted along next to me.

I ignored her.

I wrote a note to Down Below, notifying them of what might happen tonight, and slipped it into the mailbox next to the door.

Then I went to the armory, where I found Lark and Pep already at work. Most of the stuff in the armory wasn't magical, but some of it was, and Cookie had the power to turn more of it magical if necessary.

"We have to set traps," said Pep, picking up a box marked, "Top secret. Use only if completely necessary."

Once we had gathered all the useful supplies we could find, we headed back to the foyer. Cookie was there before us, dragging a large cauldron.

"Where'd you find that?" Lark demanded. "That's the fanciest cauldron I've ever seen!"

"Of course it is. My apartment has all the family's most important possessions. If it didn't, the riffraff could ruin it all. Just like in seventy-three. That might have been the pot," said Cookie. She mimed smoking as the three of us went to help her move the cauldron.

"Meaning your family?" Pep asked.

"Yeah, them," Cookie shook her head.

"What now?" I asked.

"Magical traps on all the windows," said Cookie. "If anyone goes in or out, I intend to know about it."

Under Cookie's direction we prepared Haunted Bluff Mansion for battle.

"Phew, this is hard work," said Cookie, wiping her brow. "When your mom gets back she'll either be angry or furious."

We all paused to look at the grandfather clock, realizing that the rest of the family and Grant had been gone for a long time already, given that they had expected to find the warlocks not far away from the mansion.

"Shouldn't they be back by now?" I asked.

"Unless something went wrong," said Lark.

"Has something gone wrong?" Pep whispered.

"It looks like it," said Cookie.

We walked to the window to peer out at the driveway, but between the darkness and the driving rain we couldn't see a thing.

"This place certainly looks haunted," whispered Lark.

"That's because it is," said Cookie.

Just then, the lights flickered.

"At least we have a generator," I said. "Good thing, because it looks like the power is about to go out."

When no one responded, I looked at my cousins. "We do have a generator, don't we?"

Pep bit her lower lip and Cookie shook her head. "Something might have happened to the generator while you were away."

"And you didn't get it repaired?" I asked incredulously.

"It's been on the list, but we've been very busy," said Cookie irritably.

"With what?" I demanded. "Now the power's about to go out and we're about to be attacked. The family isn't back yet and at this rate they aren't going to make it back in time!"

"They have that really good-looking man with them. I'm sure they'll be fine," said Cookie.

Yeah, but what about us, is what I wondered. I just didn't bother to say it.

We'd had one lamp on in the gift shop. Pep had tried to turn on others, but Cookie wouldn't allow it.

Suddenly, the power flickered and a great crack of thunder boomed around us.

Inky night surrounded us.

Somewhere in the haunted house a wailing commenced.

"This is wrong. They should have been back by now," I fretted. I glanced out the window, but I couldn't see a thing. Pep had pulled out a flashlight when the lights went out, but Cookie had ordered her to put it away.

"We're an authentic haunted house. We use candles here!" she hissed.

"That's a great reason to hang out in the dark," Pep sniped, clicking off the flashlight.

Cookie started rummaging around in one of the boxes she'd brought in and finally came up with something.

"Ah ha! Here are some of the old candles," she said triumphantly.

She lit the first candle by striking a piece of wood against the stone floor.

Our looks of shock were illuminated in the flickering yellow glow.

"That was impressive," Lark gasped.

"I knew you'd finally appreciate something I could do," Cookie said with satisfaction.

"She used magic to actually start the fire," Rose muttered.

"You tricked us," I accused our grandmother.

"You fell for it," she replied, and used the first candle to light three more until we each held a candle made of rainbow-colored wax.

The silence of the mansion was broken only by the pattering of the rain.

"What now?" Pep asked.

"We wait," said Cookie.

She reached into her pocket and pulled out a cookie.

"Did you hear that?" Pep whispered.

After a while, Cookie had made us extinguish all but one of the candles. We were now sitting behind the checkout counter in the near-dark gift shop, waiting. The single lit candle sat on the floor creating eerie shadows.

"No, I didn't hear anything," Lark responded. "You're just jumpy."

But then there was a sound of scraping, and this time all four of us heard it.

"The time is now! We fight for the mansion!" Cookie balled her small hand into a fist and started to stand up, but the hem of her dress caught on something and she nearly toppled over. Lark and I quickly reached out to steady her.

"Old ladies make excellent warriors," Lark said dryly.

"Who are you calling old?" Cookie demanded.

Pep picked up the lit candle and stood to her full height, which made her barely as tall as Cookie.

The scraping was getting worse. "Come on, let's go see what we can see," Cookie whispered.

We made our way toward the foyer. The rain was still coming down in sheets, and I wondered if it was possible to drown when you were on a cliff.

Suddenly all my grandmother's demands that we prepare felt like a very good idea. Overcome with urgency, I raced ahead of my cousins through the empty hallway and into the foyer.

But the foyer was anticlimactic; it looked exactly as it always had. The fireplace shed the only light, but it was enough to let us see the whole space clearly.

As we stood there in the quiet foyer, a commotion from above made me look up, only to see Uncle Taft, dressed in a full army uniform from the seventeen hundreds and wearing a sword at his side and a black eyepatch over his left eye.

He was standing on the first landing of the great staircase, waving at me frantically. "The time is fast approaching! The hour of reckoning is here! I fear that we're too late!"

"What are you talking about?" I called up to him. With a sinking feeling I understood at last that not all his ranting was crazy. In the dark, in the storm, with the threat of violence hanging over us, I had to admit that maybe, just maybe, some of the stuff he'd been going on about for weeks was actually true.

"Prepare for the Root of All Evil!" he yelled. Then he dashed away.

"Should we go after him?" Pep asked.

"Can we catch him?" Lark scratched her head.

"He knows all the secrets of this place and he has a head start," I said, still feeling the urge to dash up the stairs.

"You don't have a chance," said Cookie, stumping into the room.

"Is what he says true?" I asked.

"I'd have to have listened to what he said to be able to tell you," she informed us.

"Very helpful," I replied.

"So the noise was only Taft. Come on, we must get back to the gift shop. Do you want to give it all away?" Cookie demanded, as if the present excursion had been all our fault.

We followed her back to the shop anyhow.

"More waiting," Pep sighed when we got there.

We had barely sat down when there was a scraping sound again, but it was different this time. Something had definitely been dragged across the floor.

"Do you think that one was Uncle Taft?" I asked my friends.

"We should check it out," said Lark.

We headed back to the foyer.

"At this rate you aren't going to be hidden for long," Cookie complained. "I went to all kinds of trouble to make the Root of All Evil think we'd left the property, and now here you are parading around as if it's some kind of holiday."

"Do you want us to investigate the noise or not?" I replied.

We came into the foyer and stopped short. There was still a scraping noise, but what really bowled us over was that this time the grandfather clock was missing.

Uncle Taft had definitely not run off with it.

I looked around wildly, then cried, pointing upward, "There it is!"

Dangling near the ceiling in the middle of the foyer was the grandfather clock. The ancient, massive antique was tilted on its side and spinning slowly in the air.

Surrounding it were two ghosts, who, at the sound of my voice, looked down and glared.

"It's too late," one of them called gleefully.

"The Root of All Evil has won," the other yelled.

"Let's go!" Lark yelled, dashing for the stairs.

"I'll be right behind you," Cookie shouted as we three cousins dashed off.

As I reached the second landing I turned around to look at my grandmother. She saw me staring and yelled, "Go! I'm the only witch here who can take care of herself alone."

With that she extinguished the candle she'd been holding and the foyer went dark. Knowing there was no going back, I turned around and kept running after Lark and Pep.

After a few seconds I heard a scuffling behind us and turned to look. At first I couldn't see anything in the darkness, then the fireplace flickered just right and I made out a vampire coming toward us. Two more appeared on either side of us.

"Pep! Lark!" I cried. My cousins were far in front of me, but they were losing ground to the ghosts who were making off with Mom's prized clock.

The next instant three skeletons jumped out from a side door and cut me off.

For a split second Lark and Pep looked back at me, hesitating, but I waved them on. The clock was the most important thing.

The skeletons came toward me. The ghosts above me disappeared over the balcony.

I stumbled through the nearest door my hands could find.

"Where did she go?" I heard one of the ghosts demand.

"I have no idea. Did you see her? Did you see her?"

The ghosts were right outside the door where I was hiding. They could see better than I could, especially because they glowed, but apparently they hadn't been watching closely enough to track me. My breathing was so loud I was afraid they'd hear me, so I tried to calm down.

I moved away from the door as silently as I could, knowing I was now all alone in the haunted house.

The house had never looked so good. We sure had been ready for the big event tonight. Too bad real life had intervened.

Without realizing it when I grabbed the nearest door, I had entered The Room of No Return, which surely felt like poetic justice. A pinkish glow emanated from the overhead lights, fake blood was splattered over the wall, and a creaking sound came from the chains hanging above me. I started moving quietly along.

The next room was even worse. The vampire coffins were lined up in neat rows. Some were open, and those had plush red interiors.

There were no vampires, probably because they had scattered around the mansion looking for me.

I gulped. I didn't know whom to trust anymore.

It suddenly hit me that all the supernaturals on the property could be in on the plot; the entire field of Down Below could be part of the Root of All Evil. The basement of the mansion had always felt like another world, as in, I didn't care about them so they didn't care about me. But what if they did care? What if this whole time they had been plotting to take over the mansion from my family?

I swallowed hard. If we were to get attacked from all sides, I didn't think we stood a chance.

My cousins had kept chasing after the grandfather clock, and now I had no way of knowing where they were. My insides were twisted with worry for them.

Of all the family, only we four witches had been left at the mansion when everyone else had been drawn away to rescue the warlocks, and the (I now realized) totally predictable result was that we'd been attacked and separated.

My heart slammed in my chest.

The Root of All Evil had won.

At the very moment of my despair, though, a flickering yellow light made me pause with a glimmer of hope. But when I came around the corner into The Field of Pitchforks, I saw that the light was just part of the haunted house.

I was just headed into the next room, the Meat Cleaver Kitchen, when the feeble lights went out entirely.

Plunged back into darkness and all alone in the haunted house, I heard footsteps coming at me from behind.

Chapter Twenty-Six

It suddenly occurred to me that this might not have been the best idea. My chest started to ache and I realized that I was holding my breath. Fear permeated every bone in my body.

A stranger was in the haunted house with me. And that stranger meant me harm.

A step alerted me to something behind me, and I spun around. To my shock, there was nothing there.

I took a deep, steadying breath and told myself to go on. Standing around wasn't going to catch me the Skeleton Trio's murderer. Staying in one place just made me a target.

Another scraping noise sounded behind me, and this time I didn't bother to look. I just ran.

In the next room I halted again. I glanced over my shoulder, but once again there was nothing there. Hopefully Cookie was all right. Hopefully Lark and Pep had made some progress.

"You think you're so smart," came a familiar voice out of the darkness, a voice I had always known as lilting and friendly.

I froze.

I wasn't alone after all.

Slowly I turned around to face Mirrorz. He stood there, impeccably dressed as usual. But something about him had changed.

"Is everything okay?" I asked him.

He raised his manicured eyebrows. "Everything is splendid. My plan is working out perfectly."

"Your plan?" I asked.

"Yes, of course my plan," he snapped. "You think the rest of these fools could come up with something so brilliant?"

"At the moment I don't know what you came up with," I told him honestly.

"You'll see soon enough. Good of you to stick around. I wondered if that old kook of a grandmother of yours was lying. I thought she might suspect me. Now I can say: she was right."

My mind was rushing at a hundred miles an hour. Cookie had suspected Mirrorz? I had thought she merely told him we were all leaving so he'd spread the word to the real villains, but now I wondered if she had known all along. I certainly hoped so, but I also had to face the fact that Mirrorz was giving her more credit than I was.

"Yes, the rest of you were so busy chasing your tails and going Down Below and all that other nonsense that you didn't see what was right in front of you." Mirrorz sounded delighted.

"You mean the grandfather clock?" I said.

"Yes, we didn't have time to clean it. We'd tried to steal it before, but those ridiculous skeletons would never leave us alone long enough," Mirrorz said, shaking his head in fake sadness.

"They liked the vampires," I said.

"They didn't respect us!" Mirrorz cried.

"Given that you want to tear the mansion down, I can't imagine why," I murmured.

"Dear girl, I don't want to tear the mansion down. This is a place of great innovation, and I would never ruin it. No, I want it all to myself."

"Sure, like that's ever going to happen," I muttered. I had always liked Mirrorz. It was a shock to know how badly I'd misjudged him, and how sadly delusional he was. But I put that thought aside for later; right now I had to figure out how to get out of this mess.

"What significance does the grandfather clock have in all of this?" I asked. "You didn't just use it as a hammer, right?" I thought of the great old clock coming down on the heads of the Skeleton Trio and cringed.

"You know it's important, but you still haven't discovered why? I guess your witch's education wasn't as good as I thought," sniffed Mirrorz.

"I really hate it when people talk in riddles and don't answer questions," I shot back.

The green glow from the haunted house was getting dimmer. Pretty soon I'd be in darkness again.

"We always liked you," I whispered, suddenly feeling sad. "You were always like an older, disapproving brother to me."

"Sorry to disappoint you, but the elimination of all witches is the only way," said Mirrorz. He sounded unconcerned, not to mention impervious to flattery.

"Okay, so I guess we're not on the same side," I said.

As we talked, Mirrorz was becoming paler, and to my horror, larger. His hands started to lengthen and his nails looked like claws. I swallowed hard.

When he smiled, I knew I had to run.

"You're the last thing that stands in the way of my total magical domination," he cooed. "You'll regret ever crossing me."

"This is my home. You crossed me and you'll regret it," I said.

We'd used up all the tricks that Cookie had had us place around the mansion, but no matter. I could come up with something without my grandmother's help.

Couldn't I?

Once again I ran, and once again I dashed behind the first door I came to, which turned out to be a tiny le-haunt cubbyhole. Panting madly in the gloom, I felt claw-like hands grab my arm and I nearly screamed. But a familiar voice in my ear put me at ease. Kind of.

"It's the time of year that's important," said the urgent voice of Uncle Taft. "With the rain, all the ghosts will be at full strength, and with the full moon they'll be unstoppable. You have to smash the clock face."

"Mom won't be pleased," I whispered.

"Leave that to me," said Uncle Taft.

"Jane, where are you?" Mirrorz's voice floated over us and I pressed further back into the cubbyhole.

"I'll distract him. You run," whispered Uncle Taft.

"Sounds good," I lied.

Wait a second.

"Where do I run to?" I asked. Cookie did not seem like a safe place. To be fair, she'd probably be insulted if I thought she was.

"The Root of All Evil is heading for the roof," said Uncle Taft. He looked taller and stronger than I had seen him look in years. He was alert and vital. He was ready to fight. "You have to get there first or in the middle. I've already told Lark and Pep to head that way."

"That sounds totally doable," I said.

Not.

"On three," said Uncle Taft. Then he let go of my arm and ran forward yelling. Clearly he'd forgotten the numbers between one and four.

Sighing, I raced away from the sound of his voice and hoped that if Mirrorz caught up with him he wouldn't hurt him.

There wasn't much working in my favor in that wild escape, but at least I knew the haunted house well, while Mirrorz never came in here. He ran the house staff and thought the haunted part was beneath him.

This'll show him, I thought.

Hopefully.

I dodged around the space where I knew an old, half-burned chest stood open. When customers came through, a vampire would pop out of it and say something terrifying. I half expected that to happen now, but it didn't.

There was an emergency exit behind the statue of the scarecrow and I made for that. The door wasn't locked, thank goodness. I wrenched it open and slammed into the rickety back stairwell. For a few seconds I stood there with my hands on my knees and tried to catch my breath.

No sounds came from the haunted house. Hopefully Uncle Taft really was all right.

The staircase led all the way to the roof, and I took the old wooden steps two at a time.

I was worried, because it seemed like Lark and Pep should have shown up by now. Without them I really was all alone.

The wind rattled through the stairwell and I fought my fear as I climbed higher. Thunder still boomed as the storm raged on outside. The wind had started to lash the side of the mansion and the rain was coming down as hard as ever.

A perfect night for a haunted house to come to life.

Not that I was happy about it.

If I didn't stop what the Root of All Evil had planned now, tonight—they would never be stopped.

"Who's there?" Cookie called down. I had one more flight to go.

"It's me, Jane," I called back.

"Where have you been!" Cookie hollered.

I got close, but so much for the element of surprise.

"How many members do you think the Root of All Evil has?" I whispered to my grandmother.

"What do you think I am? An encyclopedia? Who cares? Five or fifty, they all want us dead," she raged.

"Remind me not to ask you questions anymore. I figured that given your vast array of knowledge, you might have some idea," I said.

"Don't let the act fool you. I just like watching you three run around making fools of yourselves," she replied.

"Thanks so much," I shot back.

"Don't mention it," she whispered. Fishing in her cape, she pulled out a tissue. Sparks went flying and I flinched a bit. "Thing's dusty. I really should perform spells more often."

"Please don't," I begged.

Suddenly, something brushed against my leg and I screamed for real.

Rose looked up at me with her strange green eyes. "Get it together," she scolded.

"Sorry." I was embarrassed.

"Now we really have lost the element of surprise," said Cookie. "Let's go before they do something with that clock face that we'll regret."

She adjusted her witch's hat, straightened the hem of her dress, and pulled the collar of her cape straight.

Then, without saying a word, she pushed open the door to the roof and stepped through.

Rose and I were right behind her.

Nothing could have prepared me for the rain. We were instantly soaked. A crack of lightning flashed and illuminated the roof. Even the ability to see our surroundings wasn't comforting when there were at least fifty vampires scattered around with their faces turned upward.

"You should have used a rainproof spell," said Cookie, standing there perfectly dry.

"Like I know how to do that," I said.

"Oh, bother," Cookie said, and waved her hand. Her magic sputtered and died.

The roof of the mansion suddenly seemed very high up. Gulping, I tried not to look down.

"What do you think you're doing?" snapped one of the vampires. He had stopped looking up and was now looking at us. "Always meddling. I should have known you'd come up here," he continued.

"We're going to have to jump for it," said Cookie.

"No way," I said.

"Just wanted to see if you'd believe me," she said. "We aren't going to jump. We're going to fight!"

My grandmother rolled up her tattered sleeves and turned to face the vampires, her face determined, magical chimes ringing all around her.

As her words sang out, more of the vampires took notice of our presence and turned to stare. Meanwhile, I realized that there was even more movement down on the ground. When I looked all the way down the walls of the mansion to the grass, I saw ghosts. Not one or two but hundreds of ghosts. They had all turned solid.

Now we were in real trouble. Even if jumping had been feasible, it sure wasn't going to do us any good with all those ghosts milling around down there.

Without warning, one of the vampires swung, swooshing though the air at breakneck speed. He was so fast I could barely follow him as he went straight for Cookie.

I dove forward. My magic felt slow and it sputtered as I tried to use it, but I did manage to get a basic protection spell up in front of her. There was a tinkle and a pop as the spell appeared.

The vampire was expecting a spell from Cookie and was surprised when one came from me.

We both stumbled, and the chiming sound grew. Little fireworks went off on the shield where the vampire collided with it. Cookie's eyes went wide, then narrowed.

"I don't need my granddaughter protecting me," she yelled.

I was now sprawled on the wet stones. At least the rain had lightened up just slightly.

Scrambling to my feet, I realized that more vampires were closing in, all their attention now entirely focused on us. Uncle Taft had said to smash the clock, but where was it?

None of the vampires looked like they were holding anything. Mirrorz hadn't arrived yet, but it was only a matter of time.

I thought I saw movement on one of the nearby roofs, but just as I tried to focus on that new danger, more vampires came racing at us.

"Get back to back," Cookie cried, still waving her hand crazily.

I scrambled over to my grandmother and turned my back to her and she to me. Her head only reached my shoulder, so I didn't really feel like it offered equal protection, but since I was now facing at least twenty vampires I had bigger problems than arithmetic.

"I thought all the witches left," sighed one of the vampires. His face split into a grin and a shiver ran down my spine.

"Clearly not. Two are right in front of us," said another vampire. His voice was silky and delighted. They had wanted a fight.

"Yes, it's confusing," said the first vampire. "That was my point."

"I bet you're easily confused," Cookie yelled over my shoulder.

"Cookie, be quiet," I growled.

"Can't help myself," she said.

"I believe that," I muttered.

Just then the roof door burst open and Lark and Pep stumbled through. Pep's perfect ponytail looked mussed and Lark's shoes had been singed.

Their shock at seeing the waiting vampires was written all over their faces.

When they caught sight of us they raced toward us, but a skeleton and a ghost stepped in front of them.

Just as the vampires geared up to attack again I saw Mirrorz shoot onto the roof from over the wall. He made for a corner, where another vampire handed him the clock face.

His whole expression changed once he had it in his hands. In the darkness of the night his face lit up and the pale moonlight was reflected in his cheeks. His eyes burned with delight. "Finally," he breathed.

Without a moment's thought I raced toward him. A skeleton tried to grab me, but I shot an itching enchantment at him. Both the enchantment and the skeleton giggled.

"You won't get away with this," I yelled, barreling into Mirrorz just as he was taking the clock into his own hands.

He tried to sidestep my attack, but he wasn't quite fast enough. With a thud we both landed on the ground and the old clock was tossed into the air.

Lark had followed me over and made the same diving catch for the clock that the vampire made, but neither of them was as agile as Rose. The white cat leaped through the air in a blur and landed on the spinning object as if she was surfing.

Rose perfectly changed the trajectory of the clock to send it flying away from the tumbled heap of witches and evil.

I grabbed Mirrorz by the arm when he tried to scramble away, but I couldn't keep him still long enough to perform a stunning spell. Lark was having the same trouble with her vampire.

For the split second that I was paying attention to Lark, Mirrorz took advantage and elbowed me in the rips. Pain shot through my side and I was forced to let go of him.

He scrambled to his feet and went searching for the cat and the clock.

Rose had skittered over the wet cobblestones and landed at the feet of a tall man dressed in black.

At the moment he was shimmering, and chimes like water droplets bursting were going off.

Grant stood there, but he looked different. His clothes were more splendid than before and his hat more rakish. He looked taller, too.

"IT'S HIS MAJESTY OF MAGIC! RUN!" a frantic vampire yelled out when he saw Grant.

From my prone position on the roof I tried to grasp what was happening, but I couldn't manage to take it in.

Fanning out behind Grant were several other warlocks.

Grant was His Majesty of Magic?

No way. No, no, NO way.

The man who had been staying at the mansion raised his hand and pointed at Mirrorz. The longtime butler made one more frantic dive for the clock, but he knew it was useless even as he did it.

For a split second Grant's eyes flicked to me, then they returned to Mirrorz.

"Wait, I can explain!" cried Mirrorz. Without waiting to see if Grant believed him, he then yelled, "Attack!"

All the Root of All Evil bad guys sprang into action. Overwhelmed, the warlocks and witches fought for our lives.

Suddenly, ghosts, vampires, skeletons and even the moody le-haunts came rushing through every door and window.

Mirrorz paused for a split second. "Vampires to me!" he cried. All the vampires wearing black and red gathered around him at the edge of the mansion rooftop. I told myself there was no way they were about to do what I thought they were about to do. Mirrorz's eyes swept all of us. For a split second they landed on me. Behind me was the clock. Out of his reach now.

Without a word, Mirrorz turned around and jumped over the side of the mansion. The other vampires quickly followed suit. Grant raced forward, but there was nothing he could do. When I reached the edge a split second later I saw the vampires soaring away into the blustering night.

We had saved the day, or rather the night.

Chapter Twenty-Seven

We gathered in the kitchen.

The warlocks had gone after the vampires. They had no hope of catching them, but they had to make sure they were gone. When Grant and the others left, my family and I started the slow process of assessing the damage and reclaiming our home. The mansion was in tatters after the vampires had swept through it with mayhem in mind.

No one said much at first. Debriefing would come once Grant returned. A slight knot in my stomach told me I was worried about his safety.

My mother did come up to me and give me a hug. "Are you okay?" she asked.

Lark and Pep got the same treatment from Meg.

I nodded. "Shall we get to work cleaning?"

"Not tonight," said Mom. "Let's have some hot chocolate and wait for the warlocks to return. The rest can wait until morning."

After the creepy cold of the haunted house and the freezing rain and whipping wind of the rooftop, the cozy kitchen was a welcome comfort. The fire was blazing and the smells from Audrey's cooking surrounded us. Outside, all we could see was rain.

"Can you explain what happened?" my mom asked Uncle Taft.

The old man was busy searching the corners of the kitchen. On being addressed he said, "Yes, I can."

Then he kept searching.

It was now deep in the middle of the night; Lizzie was smothering a yawn.

"Maybe right now?" my mom prodded gently.

Uncle Taft straightened. "Certainly. The Clock was the Great Clock of Time. If Mirrorz had gotten possession of it he would have been able to control time. A small step beyond that would have destroyed all witches."

"I had no idea the grandfather clock was so important," my mom said, looking stricken.

"It isn't," said Uncle Taft.

When everyone looked confused he explained, "Mirrorz thought it was the Great Clock of Time, but that had been broken years ago and never replaced."

My mom's eyes narrowed. "You mean a fake has been standing in the hallway all these years?"

"Yes," said my uncle.

"And it saved the day," said Meg.

"I'm tired," said Taft, suddenly going still.

Meg instantly went into mothering mode and led Taft away. He was swaying on his feet, all his energy used up.

We had destroyed the clock, but on the negative side of the ledger, Mirrorz and his allies had gotten away. Still, we were safe for now. We could worry about the next challenge some other day.

Audrey made everyone hot chocolate. Kip, Corey, and Cam helped while the rest of us got comfortable.

Grant came into the kitchen at last and gave us a brief report. "The other warlocks are searching the mansion. We've discovered evidence that the Root was the cause of the ghost disappearances as well. The ghosts had discovered information that the Root didn't want revealed, and the Root took care of them."

"That's terrible, but it makes sense," said Kip.

Grant nodded. "Now I'd just like to hear what happened before we got back."

I sighed into my hot chocolate. My whole body felt heavy.

"On second thought. You can tell me tomorrow," said Grant. I looked up at him and smiled.

The sprawling estate of Point Bluff Mansion stretched out in front of us. The most beautiful fall day I had ever seen beckoned, and I couldn't wait to head outside and take a walk along the water in the crisp air.

All the visiting warlocks were busy eating Audrey's delicious breakfast. I had a feeling they'd be busy for a while. In the meantime, my mom was trying to recover from the idea that she had missed the single most important event in the mansion's history.

Uncle Taft was telling anyone who would listen and a lot of people who wouldn't that he had saved the day. Most of us were starting to believe him.

Lizzie was crying in a corner. She'd been doing that most of the day. Pep said it was because she hadn't put her eyeliner on that morning.

Now that we knew Grant was His Majesty of Magic, everyone was treating him differently.

Cam looked at him in awe, while Corey kept asking him questions about training and how to become a government investigator.

I'd had hardly any time to speak with him, and I wasn't sure I cared. He had made me stay at home all week, and I was still angry about it even though I was the one who ended up having the more hair-raising adventures.

"Jane, hi." I had just rounded the corner into the library when I nearly ran into him. I backed away and scowled.

He grinned back at me, which was very disarming.

"Still mad at me for wanting to protect you, I see," he said.

"Yes," I said.

"Given that you ended up fighting the Root of All Evil for the fate of all witches and warlocks, I failed," he said. He looked terribly cute right now.

"I fought them and won, so maybe I don't need so much protecting," I said.

"You only won with help." His eyes sparkled.

I sputtered. "I was doing just fine!"

Suddenly I realized that Grant was standing very close to me. I stopped breathing. I tried to lift my eyes to him, but somehow they had become very heavy.

He took a step toward me. "You were doing amazingly. I've never seen a witch fight like that. Utterly inspiring," he said, his voice warm.

I twitched, which I'm sure was very attractive.

Then my eyes finally found the strength to look up and meet his.

Suddenly, all I could think about was kissing him.

"Grant, you're needed," Cam yelled.

We broke apart with a gasp. Red-faced, I turned away from Grant, but not before I saw a flash of surprise in his eyes.

Pity he was about to depart forever.

Epilogue

As soon as I got up the next day, I heard that Grant and the other investigators were to leave within the hour. I walked around Haunted Bluff in a sort of haze. First I went to the kitchen and picked at the muffins—blueberry, blackcurrant, chocolate chip, and carrot cake—until Audrey ordered me gone. Then I wandered upstairs, then back down.

I went outside to see Cookie, who was busy pretending to brew something yucky in her old, battered black cauldron. If I was seeking out my grandmother, I must really be in a state. Cookie looked at me as if she knew as much.

The day was blustery, and my hair and her clothes were taken by the wind as leaves skittered past our ankles.

"How are you doing?" I asked her.

She gave me a sharp look. "Fine. How are you?"

"I'm good. Sad about Mirrorz," I said, and sat down on the grass next to her.

She shook her head. "We haven't seen the last of him. You don't go naming your nefarious organization the Root of All Evil just to disappear and turn harmless after one go at enchanted clock stealing."

"I'd rather not see any more of him," I told her, suddenly feeling a chill.

Just then Grant strode around the side of the mansion with three other warlocks. They all waved as they headed inside, and Grant's gaze lingered on me longer than was strictly necessary.

I found myself blushing.

"It's a good day, isn't it? What with Grant deciding to stay at the mansion for a while and all," said my grandmother slyly.

"What?" I yelped.

"Just kidding, but I have a feeling he'll be back very soon. I'll have one of my granddaughters married yet." Cookie smirked and looked down. I followed her gaze.

"It is a good thing I got you fired from all those New York City jobs so you had to move home," she said.

I took a very deep breath. "You aren't kidding, are you." It was a statement, not a question.

"You're welcome," she said.

I did a face palm. Through my fingers I saw Cookie move.

The cauldron really was empty, and out of it Cookie pulled a wine bottle. She grinned at me.

"Just another day in Shimmerfield," she said with a toothy smile.

The End

A note to readers

If you have a few minutes, please review *Spooky Business* online. Reviews are much appreciated!

Want to stay updated?

Join my mailing list at *https://addisoncreek.wordpress.com/*

Made in the USA
Las Vegas, NV
26 April 2021

22038868R00122